C000174030

The Cathari Treasure

Daniel Arthur Smith

This book is a work of fiction and any resemblance to persons, living or dead, is purely coincidental. The characters are productions of the author's imagination and used fictitiously

.

The Cathari Treasure

Second Edition

Cover Design and Formatting by Daniel Arthur Smith

Edited by Louise Sloan

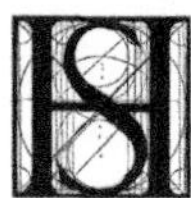

Published by Holt Smith Limited

ISBN: 0988649306
ISBN-13: 978-0-9886493-0-9

*****

For Susan, Tristan, & Oliver, as all things are.

*****

.

CHAPTER 1
NEW YORK THURSDAY 1905 HOURS

Gerard was on his way to the front bar when the man, flush in the face, had stuck his head out of the bathroom door. The man's eyes were wide locked onto Gerard's.

"Eh, there's a guy in trouble in here," he said in a rush. "I think he's having a heart attack or somethin'."

Gerard was on his way to the front bar. He was a waiter, not a paramedic. Every table in the restaurant was full and he focused on getting to the vermouth for his private party. "I'll get the maître d'," he said.

"I dunno," the man said. He glanced back into the bathroom behind him. Slowly he shook his head. "This guy's not looking so good."

Gerard sighed through his nose, took a step toward the door, and then stopped. He scanned the dining room. He needed to signal the maître d'. He spotted him across the room, facing the other direction.

Gerard pursed his lips.

"C'mon," said the red-faced man. "I need some help here."

Gerard sucked in a lung full of air. The private party

would have to wait.

He reached up and pushed the door open wide and step passed the stranger.

There was no one on the floor. "Where is he?" he asked.

"In the last stall."

He slid his tray beside the folded linen hand towels and the basket of mints, and then walked to the handicap stall at the far end of the room. He pressed his hand against the closed door, and it swung open.

With the exception of the toilet, and a large black duffel bag, the stall was empty.

"There's nobody in here," said Gerard.

"Sure there is," said the man. He slapped Gerard on the back of the neck. Hard. For an instant, there was a stinging pain. Gerard reached up and awkwardly pulled at the large rectangular cloth the man had stuck there.

"What the hell!"

The pain quickly subsided to a dull numb. The skin of Gerard's neck felt spongy against his fingertips, moved with the fabric as he tugged, and he could not feel to pinch to lift the edge of the sticky rectangle. He started to turn back, to leave the stall, but his legs gave way beneath him, and he sank into the stranger's arms.

He tried to speak, and then yell, anything, as the man walked him to the back of the stall. No sound came out, not even a gasp of air, at least not one he could feel. His throat was lost to him.

"That microneedle patch is quick acting," the man said as he eased Gerard onto the toilet. "A lot better than the transdermal patch." He propped Gerard's limp body into the corner and began to undress.

Trapped behind his eyes, the side of his face flat against the cool tile wall, Gerard watched the man remove his blue blazer and hang it on the door hook.

"The transdermal patches work like a nicotine patch," the stranger continued, "slow release."

The man crouched in front of him and unzipped the duffel. He pulled out a clip-on bow tie, and then fastened it under the collar of his white shirt.

"A real headache. The skin is a good barrier. You have to estimate when it will take effect." His tie clipped, the man opened his hands, palms up, in the mimic of a scale. "You take into account on one hand how much a guy weighs, on the other how much he ate, monitor what he ate. I mean c'mon, if a guy just had lunch, you could forget it."

The man dropped his hands to his thighs and patted them twice.

He smiled at Gerard, a long kind smile, and then sighed, stood up, took him by the shoulders, and eased him forward.

"You know, once I had to follow a guy for three hours before he got queasy, the whole time tryin' not to get noticed. On the subway, down Fifth and over to Sixth, every floor of Macy's." The man slid Gerard's white waiters coat back from his shoulders and then pulled his arms from the sleeves. He shook his head. "I swear, I thought that guy was never gonna go down." He gently rested Gerard back against the wall, this time straight back, and then adjusted his head to face him. The tile pressed flat against the patch on his neck, not cold, just there.

"Now, these microneedles are almost instant, but you know that."

He gave Gerard a pat on the cheek.

"That's because these microneedles have a microchip. A microchip and a hundred and fifty little needles." The man's eyes lit up when he said this.

The man had moved Gerard around so easily and there was nothing he could do to stop him.

He watched the stranger slip on hiss coat. The jacket fit him perfectly. Gerard wondered how this man knew his coat would be the right size. Then something occurred to him. His mind had gone muddy, but he saw it now. With the coat on, the man looked like, him. The white shirt, bow tie, and black slacks, they all matched Gerard's. The waiter's coat was all that the man needed. He needed the unique embossed dragon logo to the left of the lapel.

"These microneedles are a game changer. Altogether, I'll be in and out of here in the time it would of taken for the transdermal to even kick in. Amazing technology."

He slipped out of the stall and returned with Gerard's silver serving tray. He knelt down, removed a thermos and four tall shot glasses from the duffel, placed them on the tray, and left again. He came right back, patting down the front of the coat and the pockets of his slacks. He bit his upper lip, looked around the floor of the stall, and then peered at Gerard.

"One more thing," he said, he removed a long silver knife from his blazer, and then he knelt again, and brought out a white handkerchief from the duffel. He wadded the handkerchief into a ball, and then firmly pressed the white ball against the side of Gerard's neck. The man lifted his other arm and slowly brought the dagger close.

Gerard's eyes were all that could scream.

"Shhh," said the man.

Beneath where the man held the cloth, Gerard felt a pinch, and then his neck was warm, wet, and sticky.

CHAPTER 2
NEW YORK

Claude furrowed his brow.

"Is there an issue?" asked Cameron.

Claude drew his words out with a determined enunciation that exaggerated his already thick French accent, "I am glad to see you are back."

"I would have been here earlier. We had so many extra takes. Being a guest judge is a headache."

Claude rolled his eyes up from his cutting board, "The Food Network, they can not get enough of the Dragon Chef, eh?"

"You call a place Le Dragon Vert, you're gonna get some flack."

"You love the attention. Besides, don't worry. Everything is fine here."

Cameron knew better. Sure, Claude was glad to see him, yet at some point during the evening rush the chef was always distraught. Claude's fickle dinner hour temperament was something Cameron took in stride. Each evening started with Claude focused on some true or imagined issue.

By the time Cameron stepped into the kitchen, Claude had already begun to work himself into a fluster. Cameron picked up a towel from the counter to wipe the lens of his sunglasses and waited for his close friend's complaint of the evening.

"Well, I do not want to complain," said Claude.

Cameron nodded and smiled. Claude always started this way.

"How is the house tonight?" asked Cameron.

"The house is fine."

"Hmm."

Cameron held the lens of his sunglasses up to the light.

"It's the private party in the library," said Claude. He lifted the knife from the cucumber he was slicing then pointed the blade in the direction of the library. "That woman has been hassling Gerard every time he goes near the table."

"Right, the vegans." Cameron gave Claude a knowing glance, then grabbed a piece of the cut cucumber, and popped it into his mouth. "What's their problem?"

"No real problem. I have prepared a fabulous dinner for them, but," Claude waved the knife in a circular motion, and then continued to slice the cucumber.

"But what? Don't leave me hangin'."

Claude raised the blade again, this time wagging the knife as he spoke, "She insists on coming back to the kitchen, and you know—"

"—Don't disturb the staff," said Cameron, quickly adding, "especially during service."

"You understand perfectly. Can you please take care of it? And send Gerard back while you are at it, he is late. I have created this beautiful amuse-bouche. It is really lovely, split pea and totally vegan."

Centered on the silver tray in front of Claude a moss green liquid filled four ready-to-be-served shot glasses.

"Certainly, where is Gerard?" asked Cameron.

"I have not seen him. He must be stuck in the library

with that woman."

"OK, let me talk to them. I want that party happy." Cameron placed a hand on the chef's back and leaned into his ear, "Ms. Lacroux is a favored guest. She is from the UN, she is French, and you know she only chooses to come here because of you."

Claude grunted and went back to the cucumbers again.

Cameron went to the small corner office pleased he was still able to appease Claude's ego. Appeasing his old friend was all that was needed each evening to keep the kitchen running smoothly and Cameron gladly took on the role.

From behind the office door, Cameron took down the darkest of the three blazers he kept there on wooden hangers. He donned the jacket, adjusted his collar, and then preened himself in the small mirror tacked up on the post-it-note-covered corkboard. The haircut, the blazer, and the shirt were each part of the uniform that comprised his image, the image of a New York restaurateur. Adjusting to the image of restaurateur had taken sometime while the mindset of a uniform, a cover, was something Cameron was quite experienced in from his formative years. He often told himself he was pretending to be a restaurateur and gourmet celebrity. He often asked himself what the difference was, really.

Cameron stepped out of the office, eyes fixed and pensive, and his mind ready to start the evening, ready for the guests in the dining room. Distant by nature, he expended a lot of energy to be "on," particularly after an already long day.

"Behind you," said Cameron as he swiftly slipped past one of the line cooks toward the kitchen door.

Cameron's pace slowed to a relaxed gait upon entering the dining room.

François was polishing rocks glasses behind the bar, his back to the dining room. Through the marbled mirror tiles above the liquor shelf, he monitored the front of the house.

François was the first to notice the boss step out of the kitchen. He nodded as Cameron approached the bar. Cameron returned the nod and then leaned back on the edge of bar stool.

"*Bonsoir*, François," said Cameron. He slapped his hand on the bar.

"*Bonsoir monsieur*," François melodically sang out. François spun the rocks glass he was polishing upright in his hand then pivoted on his heel to Cameron.

"The usual?" asked François.

Cameron tapped the tips of his fingers twice on the bar.

"The usual."

The young bartender pulled the fountain gun from the holster under the bar, sprayed a shot of seltzer into the rocks glass, tossed in a lemon slice, then set the glass in front of his boss.

"Seltzer, no ice."

"*Merçi*," said Cameron. Taking a slow sip of the seltzer, Cameron swiveled his stool to inspect the house. The restaurant was loud and full. Servers glided between tables and each other, trays held to their sides or above their heads, while patrons drinking aged scotch and vintage wines conversed between nibbles of quail egg and escargot.

Cameron did not see Gerard.

He walked to the end of the short bar to get a different vantage of the room. He quaffed the rest of his seltzer and then with two fingers fished out the slice of lemon and bit away some of the sour juice. He tossed the rind back into the empty rocks glass and then set the glass out of the way behind the bar.

Cameron crossed the room toward the library but had to stop twice. Once to greet a guest's relative visiting for the weekend and once to compliment another regular, an aging actress, recently returned from a spa vacation in Switzerland. His guests loved that he remembered their names.

Cameron opened the library door. A tall black suit took up almost the entire doorframe. The young bodyguard's firm jaw stayed closed as he took a step back to let Cameron into the room. Though a bodyguard rarely stood sentry at the door, Cameron was not fazed. Guests in the library most often preferred their bodyguards to sit at the bar and pretend to read while waiting for their celebrity clients to finish dinner. Cameron initially thought the young man standing expressionless by the door either did not read or was too green to know the appropriate time to give his clients some space. Once in the library, Cameron thought differently, in the far corner stood another tall man in a black suit. Older than the gatekeeper, the second bodyguard was positioned to see out the windowed sidewall.

Cameron noticed that the bodyguards not only wore matching black suits, their tiepins also matched—emerald green, embossed with the same small design. Cameron deduced that tonight the bodyguards were not token. These black-suited men were professionals.

At the table sat the woman from the UN, Ms. Lacroux, with her guests. The small group consisted of Ms. Lacroux and three others Cameron did not know: a man and two other women. The younger of the two women looked to be around eighteen, pretty, yet plain—noticeably plain, on-purpose plain.

Gerard had his back to him and was serving.

Cameron had found Gerard, yet something was not right.

CHAPTER 3
NEW YORK

Cameron was puzzled. How could Gerard have brought the amuse-bouche from the kitchen to the library without Cameron seeing him? Cameron approached the table. Gerard was serving the wrong amuse-bouche. The shot glasses Gerard was placing in front of the guests held an orange liquid that should have been green.

Then the waiter spoke. "May I present a gift from the chef?"

The waiter's voice, his accent, was not Gerard's.

Cameron knew his staff well, and though this man has done his best to pass as Gerard, Cameron knew he was an imposter.

Cameron's eyes darted between the two bodyguards for a sign of suspicion. The two men were pillars. Cameron knew what to do.

"Good evening everyone," said Cameron. "Ms. Lacroux, if you could excuse us for a moment."

"Certainly, *Monsieur* Kincaid," said Ms. Lacroux. To her guests she said, "This is the fine young man I was talking about, the Dragon Chef. He has graced us tonight."

Cameron shrugged his brow. "You are too kind." Cameron casually sidled next to the imposter. The man wearing the white coat of a house waiter was no one he had seen before.

Cameron gently and firmly grabbed hold of the waiter's upper arm and whispered into his ear, "You should come with me. Let's step out of the library."

Cool and calm, the waiter who was not a waiter stilled himself. His ruse was foiled. One of his arms was under the metal serving tray and the other, in Cameron's firm grip, hovered above Ms. Lacroux and still held a shot glass.

Without notice or hesitation, the imposter threw his whole body into motion at once. His knees bent while the arm Cameron was holding pulled away from Cameron's grip in a downward direction so the imposter could fluidly push the tray in his other hand toward Cameron's face. Cameron let go of the imposter, then raised both arms to block and then grab the tray from his assailant. The imposter let the tray go. Both arms now free, the imposter produced a dagger from his jacket and aimed the long thin blade past Cameron toward Ms. Lacroux.

Before the assassin's blade could connect with the dignitary's throat, Cameron slammed the knife down with the serving tray.

The assassin, arm pinned beneath the tray, flashed his eyes at Cameron.

Cameron slipped his foot behind the man's legs then thrust the tray back across his chest. The assassin flailed awkwardly as he fell, landing flat on his back.

The bodyguard at the window lunged toward the table, gun quickly in hand from the inside of his jacket. From the door the younger mirror did the same. A pane in the window shattered and both bodyguards fell as bullets pierced their upper bodies. Cameron looked out the window to see a black Escalade at the curb. Out of the dark passenger window long slender fingers wrapped a silencer-capped pistol. The owner of the hand was hidden in the shadow of the Escalade. The only thing of color Cameron's eyes were able to latch onto was a gold ring set with a large garnet on the second finger of the hand holding the gun.

Another broken pane and the sound of more glass breaking followed. More shots were being fired.

"Take cover!" yelled Cameron.

Ms. Lacroux and the two women shrank to the floor. The man stayed seated, a black bullet hole burned into his forehead. No one screamed.

Dagger in hand, the assassin pushed up from the floor toward Cameron. Cameron threw his arms toward the man and effortlessly gripped the assassin's wrist. Using the man's own momentum, Cameron pulled the assassin close and off balance. Then without a breath or pause Cameron threw an arm around the assassin's head and cupped the man's chin. With a sudden twist and a crack, the assassin went limp.

Cameron had not even thought about what he was doing.

The tinted window of the Escalade closed up as the large black SUV pulled away from the curb.

"Is there a back way out of here?" asked Ms. Lacroux.

"Sure, why?" asked Cameron.

"It will not be safe to go out the front. They know we are in here."

"Right, follow me."

Cameron stood and helped Ms. Lacroux to her feet. "I'm fine. Take them," she gestured at the two women, the older helping the younger to her feet. "They are the ones in danger."

"This way." Cameron waved them toward the door of the library. There would be time to ask questions later.

At the door stood a busboy, a young Mexican named Alex. Alex had heard the breaking glass and, not realizing the glass was from the library's small windowpanes, had grabbed a small broom and dustpan from the waiter's station.

"Get Claude," Cameron told the young Mexican. "He

will need to call the police."

"No," said the older of the two women. Cameron detected a French accent, not surprising since the woman was with Ms. Lacroux.

"No police," said Ms. Lacroux.

Cameron eyes jumped between the two women and then back to the busboy. "Guard the door. I'll get Claude myself, and I don't want anyone coming into this room except Claude."

"*Si, se puede*," said Alex.

"C'mon," Cameron said to the women.

Cameron scanned the front of the house, the faces of the guests, the faces of his staff. His observation of the room vigilant, he deemed it clear. Cameron then led the two women out of the library and back through the dining room toward the kitchen. The dining room now seemed surreal, bustling with the guests unaffected by what had just happened in the library. Their adrenaline coursing, Cameron and the women could have been walking through an empty hall, their pace purposeful. He focused on the kitchen door. The women focused on Cameron.

From behind the bar, François saw Cameron's brow furrowed and eyes set.

"Everything good?" asked François.

"Yes," said Cameron as he led the women past. "Keep everyone away from the library."

Cameron and the two women entered the kitchen.

"This will just take a moment," said Cameron.

Cameron gestured to Claude, then stepped into the small office. When Claude came to the office door, he saw Cameron taking his SIG P226 9mm and a stack of cash from the safe.

"What is happening?" asked Claude.

"I don't know, but I have four dead men in the library and I need to get these two out of here." Cameron shifted his eyes toward the women now embracing each other by the worktable. "I need you to take care of the library."

The old Frenchman did not flinch. "Ms. Lacroux?"

"She's waiting for you. I'll call you in a little while," said Cameron.

Claude smiled. "Call me when you can."

Claude stepped back out of the office followed by Cameron.

"Be safe *mesdames,* you are in good hands," said Claude. He bowed his head.

"*Merci, c'est vraiment gentil de ta part,*" said the older woman. She asked Cameron, "What if there are others waiting in the back?"

"There may be. That is why we are taking the side door. After you," Cameron lifted his arm toward a door by the office.

"I would rather you go first, please," said the woman.

"Certainly," said Cameron. He opened the door and led them into a large wood paneled room. In front of them, a grand wooden stairwell led up to a balcony.

"What is this place?" asked the woman.

"This is the back lobby of the Hotel West. The restaurant was part of the hotel before Claude and I took over."

"Hmm," said the woman.

"We will be going through here," Cameron gestured to a door behind the stairs. "My car is parked in the hotel garage. I can take you home."

The older woman kept her arm held tight around the younger one as they walked into the underground garage. Cameron's black Mercedes was parked behind a concrete column not far from the door. The car chirped as he remotely unlocked the door with his key chain. The woman looked at him with disgust, "This is an expensive car."

"Let's say it's an indulgence of mine," said Cameron. He opened the passenger doors for the women.

The woman stuck her head into the backseat of the car and smirked. She stood up and helped the young woman into the backseat, shut the back door, and then sat in the front. Cameron's eyes darted over the other cars of the garage. He tilted his head, looking to see if any shadows were moving behind any of the underground garage's concrete columns. Cameron tossed his keys up in the air then caught them, circled around the front of the car and opened the driver-side door. He scanned the garage one more time and then got into the driver's seat.

"Where am I taking you?" asked Cameron.

"We are staying at Ms. Lacroux's townhouse a few blocks away, on 82nd, but that will not be safe. We can go to 39th Street, by the tunnel. There is a place for us there. A safe house."

Cameron started the Mercedes then reached to put the car into gear.

"Over there!" the woman exclaimed, pointing to the far wall.

The black Escalade was in the garage and had turned into the aisle where the Mercedes was parked.

"Duck down," said Cameron. He pulled the P226 from his waist and set the handgun on his lap then smoothly slid his cell phone out of his pocket and up to the side of his head, partly shielding his face.

The Escalade approached slowly and stopped in front of the Mercedes. Cameron did not look directly the black tinted windows. He talked into the phone, punctuating his imaginary conversation with his hands. The Escalade continued to pass, speeding up to round the next aisle.

When the black SUV turned at the end of the aisle Cameron put the Mercedes in gear and eased out in the other direction.

"Stay down," said Cameron

CHAPTER 4
NEW YORK

Cameron drove the black Mercedes out of the hotel parking garage onto the street. At the next block, he turned onto Broadway. He peered into the rearview mirror.

"It's clear. There doesn't seem to be anyone following us."

The woman slid up into her seat and turned to the back, "Nicole, it is safe."

Cameron tilted the rearview to look at the young woman. Lying on her side, head on the armrest of the door, she gazed up vacuously at the buildings passing above the car.

The young woman, dressed in a white blouse and slacks, wore no jewelry or makeup. The older woman was dressed the same, with just a little makeup on her eyes and lips and an emerald pendant low on her neck.

"Nicole, that's her name?" asked Cameron.

"*Je suis désolée.* Yes, excuse me, I am sorry. Her name is Nicole. She is my ward. My name is Marie."

"Nice to meet you Marie. My name is Cameron, Cameron Kincaid. Would you like to tell me what happened back there? Why were those men trying to kill you and why there are four dead men back at my restaurant?"

"Excuse me, Mr. Kincaid, you did not seem fazed by the shooting. You killed that man without hesitation. Very odd for a restaurateur. They teach you this in cooking school?"

"That, well, I was not always a chef."

"You were a soldier?" asked Nicole.

"Nicole, Mr. Kincaid is obviously a trained professional."

"It's Cameron, and yes," Cameron glanced up into the mirror, "I was with the Foreign Legion, but that was years ago."

"The French Foreign Legion?" asked Nicole. "You are French?"

"Yes, the French Foreign Legion and no, I am not French."

"I did not know there were Americans in the Foreign Legion," said Marie.

"Well, there are. A few."

"And you were one," said Marie.

"Yeah, well that was some time ago. Now tell me, who were those people?"

"It is complicated, Mr. Kincaid. Please take us to 39th Street and you will be rewarded. We are grateful. *Je vous remercie de tout cœur,* I thank you from the bottom of my heart."

"I understand French, and it's all right. I have to tell you, though, that I don't take well to people shooting up my restaurant."

Marie turned her face to the side and glanced up at the lights of the mall in the tall Time-Warner building as they made their way around Columbus Circle. Cameron drove along the south side of the park. Though the sun was setting, horse carriages still lined the north side of the street. In the mirror, he could see that Nicole had sat up.

She marveled at the horses and then peered down 5th Avenue as they crossed.

Marie said nothing more.

Cameron turned onto 2nd Avenue and drove quickly downtown toward 39th Street.

"How do you know how to make all of the traffic lights?" asked Marie. "They turn green as we approach each one."

"It's a trick a cabby showed me." Cameron pointed at the digital speedometer. "The lights are timed so that if you stay at twenty-nine, you will catch them all."

At 39th Street, the Mercedes turned the corner.

"Is it the townhouse up on the right?" asked Cameron.

"*Oui.* How did you know?"

"Unless those fellas are with you, the place is staked out."

In front of the townhouse, two men stood in heavy coats, too heavy for the time of year. Steps ahead of the two men another black Escalade was parked and idling.

"They are not with us," said Marie.

"Duck down until we get around the block."

Cameron drove to the corner and turned north onto 3rd Avenue. "OK, you can get up. I don't suppose there is another place I can take you."

"Not in New York. Can I please use your cell phone?"

Cameron gave Marie his cell phone and she dialed a number. He tried to hear what she was saying. Marie had turned her head toward the window and was speaking softly. When Marie finished the call, she sighed and handed the phone back to Cameron.

"So?" asked Cameron.

"This city is no longer safe for us. Is there a place we can rent a car?"

"Do you have a driver's license?"

"No."

"Then the answer is no. Where do you want to go?"

"If we can get to Boston, there are others that can help

us."

"Boston, eh." Cameron clipped his phone into the Mercedes console and said, "Phone. Call Claude."

The sound system of the Mercedes began to ring and then Claude's accent filled the car.

"Cameron."

"Claude, is everything under control?"

"*Oui,*" Claude's voice was somber. "Ms. Lacroux made a call and some men quickly came to her aid. They are cleaners, Cameron. What is going on?"

Cameron raised an eyebrow to Marie, "I wish I knew. The women are still with me."

"Uh huh," said Claude.

"I am going to be taking them to Boston. I should be back in the morning."

Marie spoke up, "Mr. Kincaid, you do not have to do that. You already have done so much."

"I decide what I do and don't do. Besides, it will give you a chance to fill me in. I like complicated stories."

"I would listen to him, Madame," Claude said over the speakers. "He is very stubborn, this one."

Marie turned back to the window. "Very well."

"Let the cleaners do their job. I will give you a call later," said Cameron.

"I intend to. Be safe my friend."

The sound system made a subtle click and the phone dimmed.

The Mercedes had reached the FDR and the city soon fell behind.

Marie and Nicole watched out the windows. They did not speak as Cameron drove.

Thirty minutes north of New York Cameron's thumb tapped a button on the steering wheel to turn on the radio. The sound of electric guitar filled the car. Marie spun her head. She reached toward the console to find the button that would stop the music.

"You must stop this, it is foul," said Marie.

"OK, OK," said Cameron. He quickly tapped another button on the steering wheel and classical piano replaced the electric guitar. "Not a rock connoisseur, I get it."

Marie crossed her arms and turned back toward the window. "It is inappropriate for Nicole to hear those sounds, that music."

"To each his own." Cameron glanced up at the mirror. Nicole continued to gaze off into the night, her chin resting on her hand.

"So are you going to tell me why we are going to Boston?" asked Cameron.

Marie did not move.

"And those men back at the restaurant?"

"They were operatives of Rex Mundi," said Nicole.

"Nicole, he does not need to know this," said Marie.

"He has helped us. To not tell him would be to lie."

Marie looked at Nicole and then at Cameron, "I will tell you, but not now." She looked again at Nicole. Cameron understood and continued to silently drive the Mercedes toward Boston.

CHAPTER 5
NEW YORK

Cameron adjusted the rearview mirror to see the rear bench seat of the Mercedes. Nicole was on her side, her eyes closed. "OK, she's asleep," said Cameron. "Now tell me about this Rex Mundi. Who is he and how do I get in touch with him?" Cameron shifted the mirror again. The lights from the car behind them flashed across his face. "He owes me for a window."

Marie checked to see if Nicole had indeed fallen asleep. She had. "Don't be foolish. Rex Mundi is not a person."

"If they're some kind of terrorist group, I haven't heard of them. Is that what they are, some terrorist group?"

"If only it were that simple. Rex Mundi is something greater. It is a force with many followers, knowing and unknowing."

"Knowing and unknowing?"

"Some are true believers and others pawns, believing they are just in their deeds."

"True believers, what the world needs more of." Cameron shook his head. "And what do they want with you?"

"It is Nicole they are after."

"Nicole? Why could they possibly want her? She's only a kid."

"They believe she will lead them to a treasure."

"A treasure?"

"They believe she will lead them to a treasure that has been hidden for 800 years. Of course they are mistaken."

"Of course. Whatever gave them that idea?"

"Somehow they found out we are on our way to Montreal. Nicole is to meet with someone important to us, an elderly woman. They believe that is where they will find the treasure," said Marie.

"And Ms. Lacroux?" asked Cameron.

"Ms. Lacroux was helping us in New York. In Boston there is another safe house and others there that will help us get safely to Montreal."

"I see."

"Do you? Because I do not wish to discuss it further. I am tired too and need to sleep." Marie did not wait for Cameron's reply. She placed her head on the back of her seat, turned to the darkness outside her window, and closed her eyes.

CHAPTER 6
BOSTON

The empty driver's seat of the black Mercedes was already washed with morning light when Marie opened her eyes. The car was parked in front of a small market. The curb was still wet from the grocer's hose and steps away tomatoes, apples, pears, and bananas filled a wall of produce racks. The shade of the market's cloth awning kept Marie cool.

She brought the mirrored visor down to check herself. She wiped the sleep from her eyes with her fingertip, then began combing her fingers through her hair. In the mirror's reflection, she saw Nicole.

The young woman sat silent in the backseat.

"You are awake. Where is he?" asked Marie.

"Mr. Kincaid went into the market to get us something to eat." Nicole smoothed the fabric of her skirt. "Is he a good man, Marie?"

"I don't know," Marie answered quickly.

"Can we trust him?"

"We will need to," said Marie. She let out a slow sigh. "At least a bit more. We are almost safe."

Marie fastened her hair back and then opened the lid of the console where the cell phone had been charging to find the compartment empty. Cameron had taken the phone with him.

Marie opened the door and stepped out of the car.

"Come, stretch your legs."

* * * * *

Cameron picked up an orange and gently squeezed it. He placed the fruit back on the stand and went on to inspect the next. His other hand fished through his jacket pocket. The cell phone had settled deep in there and could not be grasped without removing the long thin dagger he had taken from the assassin the night before. While Cameron negotiated the pocket, he placed an orange in his basket beside two others and the apples and bananas he'd picked from the produce racks outside.

He decided to remove the dagger from his inside pocket. Cameron flashed his eyes across the market to see if anyone was watching, then slid the dagger partially up his cuff. Then he lifted the dagger from his jacket, cupping the blade in his hand as he brought long knife up close to his chest. Cameron glanced down, then slowly twisted the dagger to see the detailed inscription.

Inscribed on the length of the blade was a Latin phrase Cameron could only partially decipher.

Neither hand free, Cameron balanced the groceries on a short table that was stacked with potatoes and then awkwardly twisted the hand that had held the groceries into the inside of his jacket and down into the deep pocket to get the phone. Cameron latched onto the cell with the tips of his middle and index fingers. When the phone was safely retrieved Cameron tapped the screen twice to speed dial Claude.

"Cameron, are you OK?" asked Claude.

"I'm fine. We're fine. I have them here in Boston. I

plan on taking them to the safe house and then I'm heading back to New York."

"Whoever they are, they are very serious. By the time I got off the phone with you last night the library was clean and empty. They even fixed the windows."

"Huh, I'm glad somebody did. Hey, how is your Latin?"

"Rusty, why?"

"The assassin had a dagger. I borrowed it from him." Cameron again glanced down at the blade. "It has an inscription on it that reads '*Caedite eos! Novit enim Dominus qui sunt eius.*' You know what that means?"

Claude was silent.

Cameron tilted the concealed dagger into the light, "I know the first part: 'Kill them all.' I'm not sure about the rest."

"Kill them all," said Claude, his voice soft. "Yes, I know this. In French, it is '*Tuez-les tous, Dieu reconnaîtra les siens.*' The rest reads, 'Surely the Lord discerns which ones are his,' or something like it."

"I don't think that guy was Special Forces. If he was, he was sloppy."

"This is older than the special forces. The Cistercian monk, Arnuad Amaury, said this before the massacre at Beziers. Twenty thousand people were slaughtered, in search of a few hundred."

"Beziers, wasn't that the crusades?"

"The Albigensian crusade. It was the typical frame of mind then. Rome had a policy, *Nulla salus extra ecclesium,* outside the church there is no salvation. To this day, most everyone in Languedoc knows this saying. It represents a tactic of indiscriminate massacre."

"I understand that, it's simple enough," said Cameron.

"This monk, Cameron, he was the first of the Inquisition."

"So what does that mean?"

"Nothing, I think, but someone carrying that dagger

may be some type of follower."

"The woman, Marie, said as much." Cameron twisted the blade in his hand, examining the metal more closely. "Something else is odd."

"What Cameron?"

"There seems to be blood on this blade. I didn't see him cut anyone."

"Yes, I was waiting to tell you." Claude did not continue. Cameron thought his old friend had dropped the call. Cameron was about to ask him if he was still on the line when Claude spoke again, "They found Gerard locked in a bathroom stall. His throat was cut."

Cameron hung his head. He slipped the dagger back into his pocket, picked up the basket, and then turned toward the front of the market. "I'll get to the bottom of this, Claude."

"Be careful. These people are into something very deep."

"Yeah, listen," Cameron sought the words and then changed his mind and said simply, "I'll check in later."

* * * * *

Cameron paid for the groceries and walked out of the market holding a brown paper bag. He stopped at the front of the car near Marie and Nicole and smiled. He offered Nicole the small grocery bag, "Apple, banana, or orange. Your choice." Nicole reached into the bag and pulled out an apple. "*Merçi,*" said Nicole. She then closed her eyes and held the apple in clasped hands above her chest. Nicole prayed in a low whisper and though Cameron could barely distinguish the words, he recognized the unmistakable cadence of the prayer. By the rhythm alone Cameron knew that Nicole was reciting the Lord's Prayer. After reciting her prayer, Nicole opened her eyes and bit into the apple. Juice ran down her chin and she giggled.

"So you *do* smile," said Cameron. Marie stepped close

to him, put her hand into the bag, and pulled out the orange. "*Merçi,*" said Marie. As Cameron could have predicted the corners of Marie's mouth stayed taut.

Cameron widened his eyes as he pulled the last piece of fruit from the bag. "Banana for me." He crumpled the grocery sack then tossed it through the back window of the Mercedes. He peered into Marie's eyes. Cameron chewed the banana voraciously, letting the corners of his mouth form a huge smile.

"What are you looking at?" asked Marie.

Cameron swallowed the banana. "Nicole was wrong, you don't look so bad when you wake up."

Marie glared at him.

"Do you know where we are going?" asked Cameron.

"I will need to use your phone."

CHAPTER 7
BOSTON

Using the Mercedes navigation system Cameron easily found the food co-op. Marie opened her door as soon as Cameron parked in front of the store.

"Wait for me," said Cameron.

Marie said nothing as she helped Nicole from the backseat. Cameron rounded the Mercedes, walked directly to the entrance of the food co-op, and then held the door open for the women.

The smell of sage engulfed the three as they stepped inside the shop. Shelves were stacked to the ceiling with herbs, beans, and other legumes. Middle Eastern music filled the store from a tinny metal speaker mounted up in the corner. The back wall of the shop has shelves filled with brown vitamin jars of all sizes. Fronting the length of the wall was a long wooden counter.

The building was old and the floorboards creaked with each step they took.

When they got to the back of the shop, no one was there to greet them. In the corner, hidden from the front by the racks of dried goods, was a beaded curtain to a back room. While Nicole sauntered back down the aisle browsing the shelves, Cameron and Marie stood at the empty counter and waited for someone to come out from behind the curtain. They did not have to wait long. From the back room, a skinny man came out wearing a tie-dyed T-shirt and faded jeans. His hair was short and he was clean-shaven. The man gave a wide smile to the three and then shifted his eyes first to Nicole and then to Marie.

"Can I help you?" he asked.

Cameron disregarded him. He focused instead on the long thick canvas belt that moved across the ceiling. The belt powered two slowly spinning ceiling fans. The drive motor and fans were as ancient as the building, their topsides coated with dust. Cameron had seen versions of this kind of fan in the cafes of Morocco and had thought of putting some into his restaurant.

Marie surprised Cameron when she abruptly said, "No, you do not seem to have what we need." Cameron was stunned. They'd said this was the safe house.

Marie placed her index finger on her chin then tapped. "Honey, I remember now," she said, "It was the other store that has the candles. We need to go there." She placed her hand on Cameron's arm and squeezed.

Nicole was already walking to the door.

"Thank you," Marie said to the skinny man behind the counter and then pulled Cameron toward Nicole and the door.

"Are you sure we can't help you?" asked the man.

"No, thank you," said Marie. Quietly to Cameron she said, "We must go quickly."

Cameron did not know why Marie had become so unsettled. After what happened at the restaurant, he did not hesitate to follow her lead. Nicole opened the shop door while Cameron pulled his keychain from his pocket.

As Marie stepped in front of Cameron to leave the shop, he turned his head back toward the counter. The skinny man in the tie-dyed shirt was speaking into his cell phone, his eyes pensively set on the three as they made their exit.

"Quickly," said Marie, the door not yet closed behind them. "We must hurry. They are on their way."

Nicole and Marie climbed into the Mercedes as Cameron rounded the front. Two blocks down Cameron saw a red sedan and a yellow Humvee turning the corner, neither yielding for the stop sign.

Cameron jumped into the driver's seat.

"We have to hurry," said Marie.

"I get that," said Cameron.

Cameron started the Mercedes and rapidly shifted into gear. The tires squealed as the Mercedes sped from the curb.

"How did you know?" asked Cameron.

"He smelled like you," said Marie.

"Excuse me?" said Cameron as he adjusted the mirror, his foot applied firmly to the accelerator.

"We are vegan," said Nicole. "He was impure."

"The smell of sour milk came into the room before he did," said Marie.

Cameron was aware of the phenomenon. As a soldier, he was taught that enemy combatants could easily be detected by their smell alone. When deployed he was instructed to start eating the local diet as many days before the mission as possible. There were times his squad knew a mission was coming before the orders came down simply by what the cook served.

"You were obviously right," said Cameron.

The Humvee and sedan were close behind them. The road was clear of traffic, allowing the Mercedes to race forward. Unfortunately, the other two cars had the same advantage.

A loud thump came from the back of the car.

"Mr. Kincaid," said Nicole.

"Yeah," said Cameron.

"They have guns!"

"I can see that! Get down, get down!"

Another loud thump came from the back of the car.

"Why aren't the windows breaking?" asked Marie. She was on her side looking back at Nicole.

"They aren't shooting at the windows," said Cameron. "They're trying to take the tires out. We have to lose them."

Cameron hit the brakes, setting the Mercedes on a skid that swerved the car ninety degrees and onto a side street. The Humvee started to stop too late and overran the intersection. The red sedan made the corner.

Marie shifted forward in her seat. Through the windshield, she could see they were rapidly approaching a busy intersection. "Oh my," said Marie.

"You better hold on," said Cameron.

"Nicole," said Marie, "put your seatbelt on."

Cameron braked and swerved again. The Mercedes barely missed the front of a black Range Rover. The Rover, brakes slammed, began to skid sideways. Car horns filled the air. Cameron accelerated without looking back. The Rover stopped traffic at the intersection allowing the red sedan to easily pass. The yellow Humvee was not far behind.

Cameron threw his palm onto the center of the steering wheel to alert drivers to get out of his way. The Mercedes accelerated, dodged, and wove through traffic to outrun the two vehicles that effortlessly traveled in their wake.

"We are only making the way for them," said Marie.

"Would you like to drive?" asked Cameron.

Up on the left Cameron saw the interstate on-ramp. He decided that taking the interstate would be their best chance to lose the red sedan and Humvee. To throw off his pursuers, Cameron veered to the right, away from the on-ramp. He accelerated, getting behind an Econoline van and then passing it on the right. Then Cameron cut in front of the van, darting across several lanes to make the entrance of the interstate on the far left. The Econoline made a sharp left to avoid the Mercedes. The front wheels of the van, having turned so abruptly, collapsed under the momentum. The vehicle flipped up and over, the side of the van skidding counterclockwise on the pavement in a slow spin.

"Sorry about that," said Cameron. He floored the accelerator the length of the on-ramp and launched the Mercedes onto the interstate at high speed. Cameron wove between the other cars. Traffic was getting more congested yet at the speed Cameron drove the interstate could have been a parking lot.

"This might not have been such a good idea," said Marie.

"Now, why would you say that?"

Marie pointed ahead to the large triangular tower coming up in front of them, shining metal cables skirting down from the summit. "That is a bridge, is it not?"

"That, my dear, is the Zakim Bridge, and our passage to safety."

"Oh my," said Marie.

The traffic slowed near the bridge. The Humvee and sedan were closing in. The Mercedes continued to weave between, through, and around the many vehicles at the mouth of the bridge. Across the lanes was the entrance to the tunnel that ran under the city. Cameron made another attempt to elude their pursuers. From the far side of the bridge, he swerved across the crowded lanes and towards the tunnel. A symphony of horns and screeching brakes barraged the Mercedes. The wide tunnel entrance, dark in shadow, approached quickly and for the first time Marie clenched her fingers on the sides of her seat.

The tunnel swallowed the Mercedes whole. The lights of the tunnel careened above them. If they could not tell their speed from within the Mercedes before, they definitely now knew they were moving at a reckless rate.

A torrent of shots rattled out from behind, the din thunderously echoing off the tunnel walls and deep into the Mercedes, virtually soundproof by design. In the right lane ahead a minivan sank into the pavement as the tires beneath it disintegrated. The minivan's back end swayed in front of the Mercedes, first to the right and then to the left. Cameron dodged left to avoid the minivan, cutting off a Jeep in the process. The stunned driver of the Jeep spun his wheel sharply, causing the car to upend, flip forward, and then skid along on its hood.

Cameron glanced up into the rearview in time to see the red sedan strike the back of the Jeep, launch into a spin, and slam against the tunnel wall. "I think they caused more trouble for themselves than for us," said Cameron.

"I don't think so," said Marie. She could see the Humvee circumventing the Jeep that now rested in the middle of the tunnel behind them. Another burst of shots rattled out, the last of which made loud thumps on the Mercedes. Cameron pursed his lips and shook his head. Brake lights lit up on cars ahead of them as other drivers started to slow. Up ahead the daylight gleamed above the rooftops of the cars.

Daylight engulfed the interior of the Mercedes as Cameron burst from the tunnel. He searched for an exit and at the first chance made a radical turn off the interstate.

"Ooooh," said Marie.

"German engineering," said Cameron as the Mercedes settled onto a side street. The yellow Humvee failed to make the turn and slid sideways to a stop.

"They're not going anywhere," said Cameron.

"We don't have much time," said Marie. "They know the car now."

CHAPTER 8
BOSTON

Cameron drove a few blocks before he started making indiscriminate turns down side streets. Comfortable that no one was behind them, he pulled the Mercedes up to a curb. He gestured for Marie and Nicole to stay seated a moment longer and then stepped out onto the street.

Cameron stood outside of the Mercedes with the door open, poised to jump back in if needed. He watched the corner of the street the Mercedes had turned from. The Humvee was not following. Cameron stuck his head back in the car, "Let's go, we're leaving the Mercedes."

Marie and Nicole got out of the car and followed Cameron down the sidewalk. He held out his keychain and the car chirped. In midstride Cameron stopped. He returned to the Mercedes. The car chirped again as he unlocked the door. He looked at the houses along the street, his eyes flashing from window to window in search of anybody who might be watching. Cameron opened the car door, knelt down, and then pulled his 9mm from under the seat. He tucked the handgun into his waist and then, keychain in hand, jogged back to where Marie and Nicole were waiting. Behind the three, the Mercedes chirped again.

"Where are we going?" asked Marie.

"The Orange Line," said Cameron. He gestured to the stop at the corner.

"What is the Orange Line?" asked Marie.

"The train downtown. Let's hurry."

The three walked quickly to the platform and did not have to wait long for the next train.

Cameron and the women could not keep themselves from scanning the neighborhood before they boarded the train. They stood in the center of the train car expecting someone to run up to the window looking for them. No one did. The train pulled away from the stop.

Cameron relaxed a little. Though Nicole did not look fazed Cameron could tell that Marie was unsettled. Since the shooting, Marie's manner had been stoic, but now Cameron was sensing wear.

"They were waiting for us," he said.

"So it seems," said Marie. She was staring blankly into the window.

"Good catch with that guy at the counter."

"He smelled repulsive."

"I don't think it was his intention to fool us. I think we caught him off guard."

Marie nodded her head. "I knew some of our people here in Boston."

"They must have all been compromised," said Cameron.

"I would like to think that some made it into hiding," said Marie.

Cameron looked at the subway map on the wall of the train. They were heading downtown.

Marie looked at Nicole and then to Cameron, "We need to get to Montreal. I don't know where we will be safe until then."

"I'll get you there," said Cameron.

When the train stopped at the Chinatown station Cameron led them off. "I have an idea. Stay here." He walked over to speak to the station agent. Marie could see the agent giving direction to Cameron by motioning his arm toward the exit. Cameron thanked the agent then left the station with the women.

Marie put her arm around Nicole.

The open-air markets were stocked with fish and frogs. Nicole looked curiously into each stall. Cameron sensed her dismay. He explained that the frogs were used to make dumplings.

Nicole pursed her lip. "Hmm," said Nicole, the first sound she'd uttered since they had left the Mercedes.

"Though you may not eat them, a lot of people do. They're like chicken but sweeter," Cameron caught himself, "Of course, you don't know what chicken tastes like."

"It's not a fish," said Nicole.

"No," said Cameron.

"We eat fish. Sparsely though," said Marie.

"I thought you were vegan."

"Not exactly. Mostly. Fish are part of the old tradition."

"Not impure," said Nicole.

"Right," said Cameron. He nodded.

A few blocks down the street Cameron and the women went into a small restaurant. He could tell the strong smell offended them when they shared a wide-eyed glance with each other.

The three sat at a table and ordered tea.

"So what do we do now?" asked Marie.

"We wait. A bus will be pulling up to that corner in about an hour. When it does we're getting on it."

"It goes to Montreal?" asked Nicole.

"Bingo," said Cameron. "The Chinatown bus is low-profile and puts us in Montreal this evening."

"You're going with us?" asked Marie.

"In for a penny, in for a pound."

"I don't understand," said Nicole.

"I'll get you to where you need to go."

"You will be rewarded when you do, though we have nothing to give you now," said Marie.

The waiter put three teas on the table. Marie and Nicole slid their hands around their teacups and, in low whispers, recited the Lord's Prayer. Cameron grabbed a sugar packet and ripped the end open. "That's fine for now," Cameron said to the waiter. When the waiter turned away, Cameron fixed his gaze on Marie and waited for her to finish her prayer. When Marie finished praying she matched his gaze.

"I'm not in this for the reward," said Cameron. "I would like to talk to these Rex Mundies about the damage they did to my car." His eyes flashed to Nicole and then back to Marie, "Among other things."

Nicole began shaking her head. "The Rex Mundi, there is no talking to them. Their pursuit is endless and they will do whatever they need to get what they want."

"That is enough," Marie said to Nicole. Then to Cameron, she said, "We appreciate your help, Mr. Kincaid. We need it. She is right, though. They cannot be dealt with."

"I still don't get why they want you. Who are you, really?"

"I am sorry, I cannot tell you what you want to know," said Marie.

Cameron furrowed his brow and sighed.

"We can tell him," said Nicole. "He has done so much for us already. He should know what our purpose is before he is forced to the next life."

"Forced to the next life? I don't think I am going to let that happen." Cameron winked and then took a sip of his tea. "I would like to know, though."

Marie and Nicole locked eyes and then Marie nodded.

"Eight hundred years ago the church collaborated with the Barons of France to exterminate the Cathari and take control of the Languedoc region of France under the guise of heresy. Though the Cathari were slaughtered by the thousands and thought exterminated, a few survived. They continue their beliefs in secret and protect a secret treasure. For centuries, the operatives of Rex Mundi have pursued those remaining Cathari with a continuing goal to wipe them out and take the secret treasure. The Rex Mundi believes that the Cathari treasure can transform the world."

Cameron's eyes widened, "So you mean to tell me that you are these Cathari?"

"We call ourselves *les bonnes gens,* the good people. Others know of us as Cathari. We are two of many," said Nicole.

Marie looked deeply into Cameron's eyes, "We live in secret, in the shadows, while the Rex Mundi live openly, always watching."

"Openly? When I was in the Legion, I was privy to a lot of information about a lot of terrorists groups. I never heard of the Rex Mundi."

"The followers of Rex Mundi go by many names, knowing and unknowing."

"Yeah, you said that before."

"It is true," said Nicole, "Rex Mundi is the puppet master. His agents are his puppets."

"He? I thought you said this was some kind of group?" asked Cameron.

"It is complicated, Mr. Kincaid. We, the Cathari, believe that the material world was created by an evil. This evil we call Rex Mundi. It is Latin for 'the king of the world.'"

"Right, the king of the world. Well, I don't know about that. Though there is a lot of evil in the world. I'll give you that."

"With your help to get us to Montreal, we will finally be safe."

CHAPTER 9
CHINATOWN EXPRESS

A white passenger bus with the word "Lucky" written in bright red letters across the side pulled up to the curb outside the restaurant. Cameron went out first to confirm the passage and pay the fare for the three of them and then went back to get Marie and Nicole. He led them out of the restaurant and directed them to get on the bus with the group that had gathered by the door. Near the bus, an old man and his fruit cart stood in the shade of a large umbrella. Cameron bought bananas, apples, and blueberries then joined the others on the bus. He sat in the seat behind Marie and Nicole and then from the bag of fruit he pulled a banana.

"Nicole," said Cameron.

"Yes," said Nicole. He offered her the bag of fruit.

"There is some fresh fruit in the sack," said Cameron. "We'll be OK now. I'm going to rest my eyes. You may want to do the same."

"Thank you, Mr. Kincaid," said Nicole.

Cameron smiled and tilted his head forward. Nicole returned the smile. He slipped his sunglasses on and let his headrest back on the seat. Marie tapped Nicole's shoulder and gestured for her to turn around.

*****

Cameron lifted his head off the bus seat. The back of his neck was damp from sleep. An old woman in a red vest made her way uneasily to the back of the bus. She placed her hand on the edge of Marie's seat and then, to help her balance, moved the hand to the back of his seat. Evergreens silently slid past the window. The tires of the bus hummed in a droning tranquil rhythm that was easily tuned out, leaving silence, for the most part, with the exception of a tinny noise from the too-loud headphones across the aisle and the soft murmurs of an elderly couple behind him. Nicole's head was against the window and Marie, not trying to sleep or having napped already, flipped through one of the magazines that had been left in the seat pocket in front of her by some earlier passenger.

Cameron folded his arms over the back of Marie's seat and rested his chin near her ear. "She's sleeping?" he said.

Marie looked over to Nicole, placed the magazine back into the seat pocket, and then moved from her row to Cameron's. Cameron slid over to the window to make room for her. Marie sighed as she sat and then pinched the bridge of her nose between her thumb and index finger.

"Are you all right?" asked Cameron.

"I get a little motion sickness," said Marie, still squeezing, "it caught me for a moment when I stood." She released her nose and sat upright, inhaling a large breath. "I'm fine now."

"That works?"

"So it seems. It's an old trick my grandmother taught me."

Marie turned to Cameron and smiled.

"That's a nice smile," said Cameron.

"Thank you, Mr. Kincaid. I am not a cold person. You have to understand the responsibility I have."

"If the last twenty-four hours is any impression, it would be easy to underestimate."

"It is not always like this. Sometimes yes. She knows nothing different. Nicole has lived her life in hiding, hunted. She is very strong, but I am saddened for her."

"Why is she — are you — in hiding?"

"I told you, we are Cathari, the pure ones. Hiding has become our way."

"Yes, you told me she holds the key to a treasure that will transform the world."

"You are skeptical. Why wouldn't you be? The Rex Mundi believes the treasure will transform the world. I told you they are wrong."

"That's what I mean. Why do they think she holds the key to this treasure?"

"She is destined to be a Perfect. The Rex Mundi, somehow, know this."

"She is to become perfect?"

"A Perfect, Mr. Kincaid."

"A Perfect? What does that mean?"

"The woman we are going to meet. She is an elder holy woman. She is a Perfect."

"Like a Priest?"

"She is among the holiest, but no, not a priest. More like a very holy monk."

"And Nicole is to meet this woman to —,"

"— to become a Perfect. Yes. Nicole has been trained in the discipline her whole life, and when she meets the Perfect, she herself will become a Perfect."

"Why now, has she come of age or something?"

"No, that is not how we do things. The Perfect is old and her time to pass back to the spirit realm comes soon. We travel to meet her before…" Marie held her hands up, "before it is too late."

"That makes sense."

"What does, Mr. Kincaid?"

"If the Rex Mundi know this, they probably think the

old woman is going to pass on some secret."

"They believe this to be true. New York was the first time they've surfaced in quite sometime. They will not stop until they have Nicole. She has been trained for this too."

"Hmm," said Cameron. He gazed at Nicole, softly sleeping in her seat. "That is a lot for the two of you to have on your shoulders."

"It is worth the price. Nicole is very special. To be her guardian I, too, have trained all of my life. We are prepared."

Marie placed her hand on Cameron's shoulder and smiled at him again before rejoining Nicole.

* * * * *

The southbound lane of interstate 87 disappeared when they came upon the US immigration naturalization complex, a series of gated sentry booths holding back long lines of cars, trucks, and utility vehicles. Cameron leaned into the middle aisle of the bus and saw the northbound sentry booths entering Canada clotted with as many cars and trucks. Before falling into the queue, the bus veered to the right, trailing an eighteen-wheeled livestock hauler full of hogs. Interstate 87 switched to Autoroute 15 at a large sign bearing the word "Quebec" in large letters between two equally large fleur de lis. Below, "welcome" was printed in both French and English.

The bus drove into a staging area filled with cargo haulers and other buses.

When the bus stopped, a potbellied border agent with a white beard and spectacles came aboard. He made his way down the aisle asking each passenger for their passport and their reason for coming to Quebec. The questioning shifted from English to French depending on the passport, which he stamped before hearing the answers. A couple of times he came across Canadian passengers and shifted his line of questioning to accommodate. Once he spoke in Polish.

Though Cameron could not hear all of the interactions, he was able to make out by the bursts of laughter coming from the border agent that they were cordial.

Marie clutched two passports in her hands. Cameron recognized them as French. He had French papers of his own, French citizenship was a fringe benefit of serving the first five years in the Legion. Marie closed her eyes, whispered a prayer Cameron did not fully hear, and then put the passports to her lips. When the border agent got to Marie and Nicole he did not give their passports a second look, quickly stamping them while he asked his questions, and then with a fraternal smile he nodded and offered the passports back before moving across the aisle.

Cameron had only his US passport to offer the agent. He decided his French passport would have been preferable. The border agent looked him up and down. What had not occurred to Cameron before was that he was overdressed for the Chinatown express in his blazer and slacks — most of the passengers were dressed very casually in jeans and khakis. When the border agent asked Cameron if he had anything to declare, he said no. The P226 was stowed safely in the bathroom where he'd hidden it soon after boarding. He was now certain that the handgun would be safe there. The border agent smiled, stamped his passport, and moved on to the next passenger.

Outside the bus, the driver stood by as two uniformed men inspected the baggage compartment while another circled the "Lucky" using a mirror on the end of a telescoping pole to inspect the underbody.

After speaking to everyone, the border agent went back to the front of the bus and filled out a logbook while he waited for the driver to board. When the driver stepped up into the bus the two spoke briefly. The border agent let out another brief laugh and then left the bus with a wave to a small girl in the front seat.

The bus drove around the immigration building at the north of the staging area to a queue lane made up of other buses with Greyhound and Peter Pan logos on their sides. Without ever fully stopping, the bus slowly rolled through the queue and passed the checkpoint. Clear of the immigration complex, the "Lucky" sped up to continue the journey to Montreal.

Cameron leaned forward and again folded his arms on the back of Marie and Nicole's seat. "Easy peasy."

"Easy peasy, Mr. Kincaid?" Marie raised an eyebrow toward him.

"We should be in Montreal in no time," said Cameron. He then reclined into his own seat and slipped his sunglasses back on.

CHAPTER 10
MONTREAL

The "Lucky" pulled up to a city bus stop at the edge of Dorchester Square. Cameron walked up the curb past the front of the bus. He fixated on the green dome of the building across the square, the girth of which towered over the park.

"King of the world," Cameron muttered.

"Excuse me," said Nicole.

"Cathédrale Marie-Reine-du-Monde," said Cameron. He pointed at the columned structure, the statues lining the parapet. "I always thought of this church as a mini Saint Peter's. It's basically Saint Peter's on a smaller scale."

"What do you think of it now?"

"Its name. It is the Mary, Queen of the World Cathedral. The Rex Mundi cathedral."

"Ah, I see," said Marie gazing at the basilica. She braced her elbow in her hand and tapped her chin with the fingertips of the other. "The name means nothing."

"All cathedrals are creations of Rex Mundi," said Nicole.

"You don't say," said Cameron.

"As are all things in the material world."

"OK," said Cameron. He shifted his body away from the park to Marie. "So, do you know where we are to meet the woman?"

"The person we must meet will not be available until this evening," said Marie.

Since it was still early, Cameron suggested they eat before the meeting. They went around the corner to a large hotel and entered the restaurant. After eating only fruit all day, Cameron had worked up an appetite. He ordered the salmon with a glass of wine. Marie and Nicole asked for the same.

"You really do eat fish?" he asked when the waiter stepped away.

"I told you it is part of the old way," said Nicole.

"How is that?"

"We do not eat meat or byproducts of reproduction like eggs, milk, or cheese. The old beliefs are that fish spontaneously appear in the water. So fish is allowed," said Marie.

"So the vegan thing is —"

"A religious practice concerning physical reproduction. The soul could return. We are more so vegetarians, though some such as Ms. Lacroux are vegan."

"And wine?"

"We are also allowed wine."

When the food arrived, the women prayed. Cameron waited for them to complete the Lord's Prayer and then they ate without conversing.

* * * * *

By the time they finished the meal the light through the window had turned from daylight into the amber glow of a streetlamp.

Cameron paid the bill and his companions went to freshen up.

The meal had given them new vigor and when they

walked out into the warm air the three felt at ease for the first time since New York. Along the sidewalk they passed others strolling leisurely on their way to dinner, clubs, and the late night shops of the avenue. Cameron and the two women beside him easily passed as denizens of Montreal.

They walked a few short blocks and then stopped in front of the last building on the block, a small solitary building that sat near a corner, surrounded by a parking lot.

"This is the place," said Marie.

Cameron lifted his eyes to the blue neon sign above the door. The sign portrayed a blue mermaid, her tail flashing intermittently to the left then to the right. Next to the mermaid, in fancy, stylized script were the words, La Sirène Bleue.

"The Blue Mermaid," said Cameron. "Live Jazz Tonite, featuring Glenda Johnson" was scrawled on a chalkboard in the lower corner of the window. "This ought to be interesting," said Cameron. He opened the glass door and the three entered the club.

On the other end of the vestibule, a large black man in a turtleneck and dark sport coat spread open a beaded curtain with one meaty hand and waved them through with the other.

The sparsely crowded La Sirène Bleue had been decorated in the fifties or sixties. Patina and shadows accented the brown wood and brass detailing the room. The namesake, a topless mermaid with a blue tail, orange hair, and perky smile, was depicted on a mural that ran the length of the sidewall. The blue mermaid rested on a rock outcropping surrounded by a turbulent seascape. A martini glass in her hand held an obligatory olive complement.

On the other side of the room huge aquariums, their algae-crusted backs painted cerulean blue, sat above the shelves of liquor on the wall behind a long bar. The aquariums may have held salt-water fish at one time. Now old, oversized cichlids, mostly blood-bellied Oscars, inhabited them.

In the back of the room a double bass, baby grand, and small drum kit were being put to use by three leathery-faced musicians. The bass player sported a goatee that ran pencil thin on the sides and a tall porkpie hat high on his forehead. His elongated face paralleled the neck of the double bass he was gently plucking. The piano player and drummer each moved in slow time to the lament of the torch song crooned by the beautiful caramel colored mezzo-soprano.

Glenda Johnson stood in low blue light on a small corner stage. Her song of love and lovers was sweet and slow and she sang the ballad deeply. Like the trio playing with her, Glenda performed with her eyes closed. Her head tilted slightly to the side as she sang a passionate declaration that true love is unstoppable.

Cameron could not help being mesmerized. He did not immediately notice when the woman in the blue cocktail dress, menu cards in her hand, sidled next to them. When he did, she gestured to Cameron and the women to follow her. The woman led them to a small round table near the stage, and placed the menu cards on the table when they sat.

"*Trois vins rouges, s'il vous plait,*" said Cameron.

"*Oui, un instant,*" said the woman in the blue dress.

The three quietly listened to the performance as the woman went to get the drinks from the bartender. She quickly returned with wine and a small crystal bowl of assorted nuts.

When the song ended, the audience applauded and only then did Glenda open her eyes. She nodded her head to the crowd, if so sparse a group could be called a crowd, and placed her hands together, graciously thanking the room.

The bass player took a long draw from a rocks glass and then, refueled, began a driving rhythm. The piano player and drummer bobbed their heads in time and launched into an upbeat standard. Glenda looked over to the band with a full open smile, said something Cameron did not make out, and then turned back to the microphone and belted out the verse.

Glenda engaged the room and at one point in the song, locked eyes with Marie. Cameron sensed a recognition that was confirmed when the singer's eyes trailed to Nicole. In a brief gesture, Glenda lowered her head to the young woman.

The light shined in Marie's eyes. Her hand lightly tapped the table in time with the bass.

"Glenda? We're here to meet Glenda Johnson?" asked Cameron. Marie nodded.

CHAPTER 11
MONTREAL

Cameron felt relief, maybe because they had arrived at their destination, maybe because of the wine, perhaps both. He eased back in his chair and lifted his glass. When Glenda's eyes met their table again, Cameron tilted his glass toward her and she responded with a smile.

When Glenda finished the song the room applauded again and she excused herself from the stage. She stepped over to the musicians, said something, and then joined the three at the table. Marie stood and the two embraced tightly.

"*Mon amie, tant de temps,*" said Glenda. The two traded kisses on each cheek.

"It has been too long," said Marie, holding Glenda close to her.

When the two let go, they stepped far enough away from each other to trade an inspection. "*Si belle,*" said Glenda.

"*Et tu,*" said Marie. She gestured toward the table, "Glenda, you remember Nicole."

"Of course, what a lovely woman you have become."

"*Merçi,*" said Nicole.

"And this is Mr. Kincaid."

Cameron stood and held out his hand. Glenda placed her hand on his.

"How do you do, *monsieur*?"

"I'm well, thank you. Your singing is lovely."

"*Merçi,* I am glad you enjoyed it."

Glenda's brow furrowed, very slightly, subtly. "Mr. Kincaid, are you a good man?"

"Excuse me?" asked Cameron, unsure what she meant.

"She is asking if you are one of us," Marie said to Cameron, and then turned back to Glenda. "No, he is not. But he has gone out of his way to help us."

Glenda's face lost expression.

"He can be trusted," said Nicole. With that, the smile returned to Glenda's face and she gestured Cameron to return to his seat.

"After you," said Cameron.

All were seated, Glenda taking the seat between Marie and Cameron.

"I am sorry, Mr. Kincaid. It seems I, we all, owe you a debt. In these times it is hard to know who to trust."

"I understand," said Cameron.

Glenda placed her hand on Cameron's and gazed into his eyes.

"Glenda and I grew up together," said Marie.

"Really," said Cameron.

"Yes," said Glenda, "hard to believe that so many years have passed." She looked across the table at Nicole. "The Perfect will be glad to see you."

"Is she near?" asked Marie.

"She is not. The Rex Mundi has been close — too close. It was not safe for her here any longer. I know you have had some trials of your own, but it is not safe for you either." Glenda raised her head and scanned the room. "They watch us even now."

Cameron faced the length of the room from his side of the table. He could see two men in leather jackets at the bar, conversing amongst themselves, and stealing glances between Glenda and the table. Under the mural, a man and a woman shared an iced bottle of champagne from a bucket next to their table. They, too, kept glancing at the table. He had not thought about anyone in the club being an assassin before Glenda said they were being watched. Now every patron looked suspect.

"Who is it?" asked Cameron.

"Any of them, all of them. Hard to know," said Glenda.

As Glenda and Marie talked amongst themselves, Cameron continued to size up the patrons. When his eyes got back to the large man at the door, three men entered the club. They were young, their haircut close to their scalps, and all were leather clad. The leather jackets were not out of the ordinary. Many of the men Cameron had seen on the streets of Montreal as well as a few here in La Sirène Bleue sported them. Dark leather jackets were always in fashion in northern cities. Something about these three men stood out to Cameron, though, and made them different than the others around them. Their grooming, their trained physiques, the way they postured at the door, all three together, not one with his back to the room. These men were military — that Cameron was sure of. Two of them conversed with the doorman while the third, the tallest of the three, scanned the room, ultimately locking his eyes on Glenda. The tall man placed his hand on the shoulder of the man standing next to him and whispered into his ear. This one then looked to the end of the room, past the table where the four were sitting, and then back to the tall man. He nodded his head and began to walk toward the table.

Cameron was sure something was up. He leaned into the table to casually slide a hand beneath so that he could secure the P226 tucked into his waist.

"Excuse me," Cameron interrupted Marie and Glenda, "this guy coming up behind you and his buddies at the door don't sit right with me."

Glenda did not turn toward the door. She looked passed Cameron to the bass player. The player acknowledged Glenda's concern with a nod. "It seems Tom agrees with you, Mr. Kincaid," said Glenda.

As the young man approached the table Cameron's hand tightened on the P226 grips. The young man walked past without a glance down to the table or anyone sitting at it.

"He is going to the men's WC," said Marie.

At the edge of Cameron's peripheral vision, he saw that was so. Marie turned around to look at the two men standing sentry at the front door. "They are only waiting for their friend," said Marie. "They will be leaving soon."

Cameron wanted to believe Marie. Though the two at the door no longer scanned the room, something was still not right with them. Cameron knew he was correct that they were military. That was not what stuck out, though. What bothered Cameron was the way they stood. The music the Jazz trio played was infectious with a solid backbeat and everyone in the club was bobbing their head, tapping their fingers or feet, or all of the above. Not the two at the door. They stood poised. Only one other person in the club was still, set for recoil, unaffected by the music, and that was Cameron himself.

A moment later, the young man exited the men's room and walked back by the table as he had the first time, without a glance to any of the four. Cameron gripped the P226 firmly. When the man got back to the front door where the other two were waiting, all three left the club.

Marie watched the door close behind the last. "You see," said Marie, "only using the WC."

Cameron was still unsure about the three and Glenda confirmed his suspicion. "They have been here before," she said.

"That was a sweep," said Cameron. "They were casing the room. They'll come back and when they do they'll mean business."

"Mr. Kincaid is right. It will not be safe to leave through the front. Come," Glenda stood, "follow me to the back. You can leave that way."

The three followed Glenda through a door behind the stage to a small musty back room used for storage. Cases of liquor lined one wall and a large metal washtub with a mop set inside was on the other. Cameron decided the musty smell was coming from the mop. At the back of the room was metal door.

Glenda reached behind a box of candles on a low shelf and brought out a black handbag. She removed an envelope, "Take this," Glenda said to Marie. "The Perfect is in Toronto. The address is here along with some cash."

Glenda took hold of Marie again and the two held each other in another tight embrace.

"When this is over I will be back to see you, *mon amie,*" said Marie.

"It will be like the old days," said Glenda. She then hugged Nicole, wished her well, and lastly turned to Cameron and took his hand between both of hers. "Please be safe Mr. Kincaid. We all thank you for this."

Cameron did not know what to say. He had thought his journey over until a few moments before. "I will," was all he said.

Glenda unlocked the metal door.

"*Au revoir,*" said Glenda, and closed the door behind the three as they stepped out into the night.

CHAPTER 12
MONTREAL

"We should move quickly," said Cameron. He led Marie and Nicole into the parking lot behind La Sirène Bleue. "We can go back to the hotel and plan our next steps from there."

From a tall pole, two halide lamps shone down on the almost vacant lot. Cameron peered into the far shadowy corners. He saw no signs of life. If the three young men were waiting for them, they were on the main street in front of the club.

"This way," said Cameron. He lifted his hand toward the side street that ran along parking lot. "We can circle around the block."

The three passed the few cars in the rear of the parking lot and were stepping onto the sidewalk when a blast lifted them into the air and thrust them forward. For a split second, thunder surrounded them and then silence. Bright yellow light flooded the dark side street. Cameron scrambled to find and shield the two bodies on the curb. Nicole squeezed her head between her hands, her eyes pinched closed. Marie was yelling something at Nicole that Cameron could not immediately make out. A ringing came into his ears and he began to hear Marie's pleas, at first muted then, as quickly as sound had escaped him, he could here what she was yelling: "Nicole! Are you OK? Are you OK?"

Cameron brought himself up to his knees and ran his eyes across each of the women, head to toe. They were OK. The corner of the building had shielded them from the worst of it.

Marie wrapped her arms around Nicole. "*Nicole, ouvrez vos yeux, ouvrez vos yeux!* Open your eyes, let me see you!"

Nicole did open her eyes, leaving her hands on the sides of her head. "What happened?" asked Nicole, "Everything was so loud, then no sound."

Cameron helped them to their feet, "It was the club," he gestured back. "They blew up the club."

Marie now realized for the first time that La Sirène Bleue was in flames. She put her hand on Cameron's shoulder to push him aside. "Glenda. We have to go back." Cameron put his arms around her and held her, shielding her from the fate of her friend. She pushed at his chest with her forearms. "We have to go, she needs our help."

"There is nothing we can do," said Cameron. "We have to get out of here."

Nicole was composed. She took Marie by the shoulders and pulled her back toward her. "Mr. Kincaid is right. She has gone to the next life. We must go."

Marie pulled her arms from Cameron's chest and pressed her wrists against her forehead. "You are right," said Marie. Her tone lowered, her hysteria passed. "We must go."

Cameron turned back to view the burning building. Two more smaller explosions murmured from within the club, the second causing a tall flume to shoot out above.

"I don't see anybody. They must think we were in the club. Let's go now before they start snooping around."

CHAPTER 13
MONTREAL

"Are you back in the city?" asked Claude.

"I am in a city, all right, but not New York," said Cameron.

"Oh, you are still in Boston."

"Actually, I left Boston, and my Mercedes, this morning."

"So where are you?"

"Would you believe I'm walking the streets of Montreal?"

"I love Montreal. What the hell are you doing there?"

"The hits just keep on coming. After I talked to you in this morning in Boston..."

Claude had answered the phone expecting Cameron to tell him he had returned to New York. Cameron explained to him that was far from the case. As Cameron led the women along the side streets toward the hotel he briefed Claude about the skinny tie-dyed man, the car chase across the Zakim Bridge, the bus ride to Montreal, and then finally the fate of Glenda and La Sirène Bleue. Then, as Marie and Nicole whispered prayers by his side, Cameron told Claude what he knew about what he had been drawn into.

After hearing Cameron's account of the day's adventure, Claude was momentarily silent. Then Claude asked, "All of that since we spoke this morning?"

"I tell you, what happened here was exactly like what happened to us in Tangier ten years ago," said Cameron.

"I don't like the sound of this Rex Mundi, and I think you are right, it all sounds too familiar. This all adds up to only bad news," said Claude.

"I'm sure you're right, but I gave Marie and Nicole my word that I would get them to safety. I need to see this through to the end, whatever that means."

"It might mean your end, my friend. My advice to you is to tread lightly." Cameron heard Claude sigh, and then Claude continued, "Can I help you? Would you like me to come to Montreal?"

"Thanks, Claude, you don't need to come up here. I need you to keep things together until I get back."

"Of course."

"There is one thing you can do, though," said Cameron.

"I will call him," said Claude, "as soon as I am off the phone with you."

"Ha, ha. You don't miss a trick."

Claude knew that Cameron needed Pepe, a friend from their time together in the Legion. Pepe lived in Montreal and Claude could easily find most anyone he and Cameron had served with.

"Find a safe place to wait for the call," said Claude.

"Thanks Claude. I'll hang tight until then."

Cameron finished the call and then looked at the battery indicator on his phone. The Mercedes charged the cell phone's battery when the phone was plugged into the car. Cameron did not have another way to charge the phone and now, a day out, the battery was already half gone. Cameron decided he would wait for the call from Pepe and then go silent, using the phone sparingly until he needed to reach out again.

The sound of sirens filled the streets as emergency vehicles fleeted to the remnants of La Sirène Bleue. Cameron, Marie, and Nicole had walked three blocks away from the club before circling back downtown toward the hotel to wait for Pepe's call.

Though the day had been long, the evening was still young. Back on the avenue, couples and small groups were as they had been when the three had left the hotel so pleasantly only a short time before.

When they walked into the lobby Marie, wide-eyed and jaw open, took in Cameron and Nicole under the light. "We look a mess," said Marie. She reached up and tucked Cameron's shirt collar back below his blazer. "Shall we meet in the restaurant?"

"That would be fine," said Cameron. He forced a smile back at Marie and Nicole, not only for their sake, but also for his own. "I'll see you in there in a few minutes."

CHAPTER 14
PEPE

With a swagger and a nod to the hostess, Pepe Laroque entered the hotel restaurant. He proceeded to the table in the back of the restaurant where the light was lowest. Cameron, Marie, and Nicole were at the table waiting for him. As Pepe approached the table, he opened his arms to Cameron. "*Mon ami* Cameron," said Pepe in his deep French accent, and the two embraced and traded kisses on each cheek.

"Retirement is treating you well, my old friend," said Cameron. He was referring to the paunch Pepe had developed that was mostly hidden by his black sweater and sport coat. Pepe was not fat, but his short height betrayed his widening girth.

"It is a good life," said Pepe, placing both hands on his belly. "We cannot all be eternally trim, like the Dragon Chef."

Cameron brushed his finger across his nose. "You heard that."

"I heard."

Cameron gestured to the table. "May I introduce Marie and Nicole," he said. "Marie, Nicole, this is my dear old friend Pepe."

"*Bonsoir, Monsieur Pepe. Je suis heureuse de vous rencontrer,*" said Marie.

"*Bonsoir,*" said Nicole.

"*Bonsoir Mesdames. Enchanté,*" said Pepe, a gleam in his eye. "Let us just say I am a dear friend, not so old."

"Have a seat," said Cameron.

"You have picked rough company," said Pepe as he took his seat.

"I kind of fell into this," said Cameron.

"I was speaking to the ladies." Pepe raised his eyebrows and leaned slightly toward Marie and Nicole, "Beware of this one, I tell you. In all of the years I have known him, he is never far from falling, it seems."

Nicole giggled at Pepe's exaggeratedly cavalier manner and Marie kindly released a subtle smile, a compliment on her part.

Pepe waved over the waiter. "*Garçon, une autre carafe de vin s'il vous plait,*" said Pepe and then, having ordered wine, he was quick to business. "When old Claude called I was expecting that you or he would be in town for a visit. Then I said to myself, Pepe, it is something up with Kincaid. And to be sure." Pepe opened his eyes wide.

"So Claude has filled you in?" asked Cameron.

"I know nothing really. I do not want to know." His pleasant grin shifted to a sneer and his tone to low and sarcastic, "But I did like that little jazz club that disappeared tonight."

Marie dropped her eyes to the table. Pepe squinted at Marie, pursed his lips, let the corners of his mouth turn up, and then said, "But a little adventure is good for the blood." Pepe winked at Cameron. "Anything you need my friend."

The waiter brought over a carafe of wine for the table. "*Merci,*" they each said softly, almost in unison.

Cameron raised his glass to Pepe. "There really is nothing to tell. Not now, anyway. But we need to get to

Toronto, and we need your help."

Pepe slipped his hand into his sport coat, produced a set of keys and a ticket to the hotel garage, and placed them on the table. "Take my car," said Pepe. "It's a Chevy. It is not as nice as your Mercedes, if I remember. But it will serve you nicely."

Marie pulled the envelope that Glenda had given her from her handbag. "How much do you need? We do not have much but it is all for you if you like."

Pepe held his palm to the envelope. "Please," he said. "You I forgive. Cameron knows better." He reached back into his jacket pocket, pulled out a small notebook, and tore away a page. He held the paper up with one hand and fiddled with the key ring on the table with the other. When Pepe found the key he was looking for he dangled the key ring next to the paper. "This is the address to a cabin I have on Lake Ontario, and this round key opens the side door. Stop there on your way to rest for the night." He looked at the three of them and then under his breath said, "It will do you some good. You look like you need it."

"*Merci, monsieur,*" said Marie.

Pepe smiled, toasted them with a nod, and then took a drink. "Under the seat you will find a friend."

"I have a gun," said Cameron.

Pepe chuckled. "Of course you do. Only you would bring one across the border in these times." Pepe's eyes went stern. "One can never have too many." Cameron nodded his head in agreement. Their long shared history in the Legion had taught them that armament was not something to be missed when needed.

When the wine was finished, Pepe walked them to the door. "If you need anything call me, and try to return my car in one piece."

"You are a true friend, Pepe."

Pepe grabbed Cameron's shoulders and placed a kiss on each cheek. "Vive la Légion."

Cameron peered deeply into Pepe's eyes. "The Legion

is our strength."

CHAPTER 15
HIGHWAY 401

Pepe was right in that the old Chevy was not the Mercedes. The numbing hum of the engine muted out all else in the car. Pepe was also right that Cameron had always put himself close to trouble, inviting trouble by daring convention. Few Americans join the French Foreign Legion and Cameron had been one of them.

Apart from French officers, only a quarter of the ranks of the French Foreign Legion are French. The rest are foreign nationals from countries such as Bosnia, Germany, England, and even the United States of America. The romantic idea of adventure-seeking may be the draw for some, and the idea of running from something is appealing to others But the harsh realities of the Legion weed out all but elite professional soldiers, who are signing on for the esprit de corps unique to the organization or for the chance of citizenship awarded after five years of service.

During candidate selection in Aubagne, Cameron pushed for a position in Corsica, home of the elite Second Foreign Parachute Regiment. Merely to try out for the elite unit meant signing a longer hitch in the Legion with no guarantee of being accepted in the regiment, but that was of no consequence to Cameron. Though the training almost killed him, still he landed a dragon badge, and if he was looking for trouble there was no shortage during his time as a commando.

Marie and Nicole were both asleep before they escaped the lights of the Montreal. Cameron tilted the rearview mirror to check on Nicole. She was sunk down in the back seat, her head tilted against the armrest at an impossible angle.

Gazing at the young woman — barely a woman — sleeping in the backseat, Cameron knew he was far removed from the covert operations of his days as a soldier. Those years and that life were put behind him when he moved to New York and opened Le Dragon Vert with Claude where he would become known as the Dragon Chef.

This was a new kind of trouble and Cameron was not sure that he understood. He asked himself why these people were after such a sweet young woman. What kind of treasure could be driving such madness? And the Rex Mundi themselves, why had he not heard of them before? He thought back. Maybe he had confronted the Rex Mundi under another name, another guise. He certainly performed many missions against questionable shadowy groups and clandestine men. Cameron himself was not alien to the fervor of cult mentality. "Vive La Légion, the Legion is our strength." Cameron had accepted a role some would call mercenary and never wasted a moment on the moral hazards of his actions. To dwell on the morality of his actions, to question his orders —he never saw the point. He always believed he was fighting the good fight. He felt that way now. Cameron knew in his heart that he was one of the good guys. To Cameron that meant that if the Rex Mundi were fighting the bad fight, they were the bad guys. Though Cameron may have left the Legion, he felt as compelled now as ever to fight the good fight, to defeat the bad guys like the Rex Mundi. That much remained the same.

* * * * *

About four hours out of Montreal, Cameron saw an exit for Highway 25. He turned off the freeway and drove south. Marie stirred and then woke under the streetlamps of a small-town main street. She had awoken several times over the past few hours, never quite comfortable enough to stay asleep. Neither Marie nor Nicole had asked to stop. Cameron was thankful for that.

"Where are we?" asked Marie.

"The sign said Colborne. We're getting close," said Cameron. He handed Marie the scrap of paper containing the directions and she helped navigate the next few miles of short turns and dirt roads.

Marie could not easily make out Pepe's notes. She held the paper down by the light of the ashtray and tried to decipher the last few scrawls. Cameron put his finger on the paper and pointed at a small straight line, "I believe that is a 'L,' meaning left," said Cameron.

"Then why is it not like the others?"

Cameron moved his finger back to the line above to see what was written.

"Look out!" yelled Marie.

Cameron looked up to see two golden eyes just ahead of them, flying toward the car. Cameron hit the brake and the back of the car slightly fishtailed, stopping in front of a large deer standing in the middle of the road. The deer looked across the road, back at he car, back across the road, and then sauntered away.

"Whew," said Cameron, "That will get your heart pumping."

"Nicole," said Marie. She turned to the backseat.

"She is still sleeping," said Cameron. "Didn't even flinch."

Marie put the paper back under the dashboard light. "So, the next turn is a left, I think."

Cameron drove more slowly and let his eyes sneak out into the woods in search of any other creatures that may decide to traverse their path. Soon they made the last of the turns and came to the entrance of a two-track trail.

The cabin appeared as a brown wall at the end of the two-track. Cameron turned off the engine and left the headlights on. The engine terminated to a sudden stillness. Cameron sat in the quiet, feeling numb. His eyes were glazed and he wanted a shower. Nicole, still half asleep, leaned forward.

"We're here," said Marie.

The car doors opened to a sweet rush of cool air. The sound of Lake Ontario crashing upon the shore echoed through the trees around them. They had not seen the lake from the main road and it remained hidden from view.

Cameron got out of the car, and then went to the cabin door. The key on the ring slid in easily. He stepped back to the car and killed the headlights.

The cabin was backlit by the moonlight flooding the trees on either side.

"OK," said Cameron. "Let's head in."

"Can we see the moon first?" asked Nicole.

"Why not?" asked Cameron.

The three walked toward the lunar light at the side of the cabin. Turning the corner, they were instantly struck by the large waning moon floating above the sea of Lake Ontario. In front of the lake, the crashes and ebbs were clearer, louder, and the light breeze was moist against their cheeks.

"It's beautiful," said Nicole, "it's like an ocean."

"Yeah, it's one of God's amazing creations," said Cameron.

"But it's not," said Nicole, and she turned back toward the door of the cabin.

CHAPTER 16
LAKE ONTARIO

Their arrival at the cabin invigorated them. The southern glass-framed wall that faced Lake Ontario spanned the two stories of the shaker frame, the bedrooms recessed on the balconied second floor above the kitchen. The hearth sat on the sidewall, the large stone chimney dwarfing the room. Cameron had a secret dread that a large game head would be mounted on a wall or that a bearskin would drape the balcony, but neither was the case.

The cabin was only remote in the sense that the property was away from the highway. It was still connected to the grid. The lights flicked on with a switch. The natural gas stored in the large tank out by the shed would need to be turned on for hot water and cooking. Cameron turned it on as Pepe had instructed while Marie and Nicole prepared the bedrooms upstairs.

When Cameron yelled up to tell them that the gas had been turned on, he found Marie and Nicole were already at work washing away the last few days travel.

Cameron opened the fireplace flue and quickly prepared a fire with some of the chopped wood that was stacked neatly along the stone wall. The dried wood ignited without much effort. Cameron placed some larger pieces over the flame and then went into the kitchen.

The pantry consisted of a small walk-in area off the kitchen with shelves lining three walls top to bottom. Cameron pulled the weighted string that hung in the center of the room, illuminating a bare bulb attached to the ceiling. The contents of the pantry were shelved in an orderly fashion. Grains and pastas filled an entire shelf, large cans and bottles of juice and water lined the top, and an array of canned goods covered the bottom shelves. Considering Marie and Nicole's dietary restrictions, the choices were ample. He took down some pasta and olive oil and found cans of tomatoes, potatoes, white beans, and spinach. He took them over to the counter and then opened a large cupboard door where he thought he would find pots and pans. Cameron was right — they were inside, plus an item he did not expect. A large mustard-yellow clay cone capping a matching pot sat centered on the front of the shelf. Cameron had forgotten Pepe's adoration for Moroccan cuisine. That there would be a tagine in Pepe's cupboard should have been no surprise.

Cameron returned to the pantry, swapped the pasta for a bag of Israeli couscous, and then gathered an array of institutional-sized containers of cayenne, curry, paprika, and salt. He turned on the oven to preheat and went to work.

At the end of the counter, a small, portable cassette deck was plugged in the wall. On top of the deck were cassette tapes. Cameron thought them antiquated and did not expect much in way of music when he flipped through them. He did not know the artist on the first two cassettes. The last he recognized: Pavarotti. The cassette slipped into the player and the small door snapped shut tightly. With a stroke of the play button, the tenor's voice filled the kitchen.

* * * * *

Marie and Nicole came down to the main room. The

dim amber light of the fire accented the furnishings and through the tall glass, the waning moon shined. The soft smell of cumin, nutmeg, and cinnamon lingered over the smell of the burning wood.

Cameron reclined on the large sofa with one leg up on the edge of the long coffee table. In his hand he held a glass of red wine.

"You look refreshed," he said.

Marie and Nicole had found sweat clothes that fit well enough and their heads were so tightly wrapped in shaggy towels they reminded Cameron of turbans he had often seen men wearing behind the wheel of the New York yellow cabs.

"We left plenty of hot water for you," said Marie.

"That sounds good," said Cameron. He gestured to the table. "There is wine on the table and the food is about ready." A bottle of wine stood between two small tea lights and three stations of plates, silverware, and placemats.

"Very proper, Mr. Kincaid," said Marie.

Cameron placed another log on the fire, jabbed the wood into place with the iron poker, and then walked toward the staircase. "Relax," said Cameron. "I'll be five minutes, and then we can eat."

* * * * *

With the trials of the last few days, the fact that Cameron was a New York chef had slipped Marie's mind. She had never actually had a chance to eat anything at the restaurant to build an impression. Up until now, her thoughts of "Mister Kincaid" were of his experience as a mercenary — a retired soldier. Marie's thoughts were reinforced by actions that made her feel safe in his company. Now she was reminded that his past profession had been put aside for his new vocation. The presentation was impressive.

After the Lord's Prayer, dinner started with a full, fruity

Spanish wine from Pepe's wine cave. With that wine, Marie could have washed down most anything, edible or not. Still, Cameron astonished her. Though this was not the first time Marie had eaten a stew from a tagine, this was the last thing she expected to see on the table. When Cameron removed the heavy clay cone, a steam ripe with cinnamon and cayenne misted the table. The large pearls of couscous, marbled with spice, formed a thick base across the platter. Potatoes, tomatoes, and spinach symmetrically covered the field in a colorful, ornate design.

"This from tins?" asked Marie.

Cameron flashed a wink. "One more thing."

Cameron picked up a wide spatula, and then opened the door to the oven. He thrust the spatula under a large ball of foil and managed to keep it balanced as he walked from the oven to the table, finally letting the ball rest on a plate next to the wine. His arms then hovered above the ball, hands bent forward, rattlesnakes ready to strike. Decisive and quick, he snapped both hands forward, grasping the edges of the foil, and then curling his index fingers back towards his thumbs. Each time his fingers met the hot foil he blurted a word: "Ta, Ta." The first attempt set free a fold that held the foil together. A second strike pulled the foil back, unveiling a browned loaf of bread.

Marie and Nicole both clapped.

"Mr. Kincaid," said Nicole, "this looks amazing."

When Cameron took his seat, Marie raised her glass to him, "To the chef."

"Thank you," said Cameron, accepting the toast.

"*Pain frais,* how nice," said Nicole.

"How were you able to bake bread so fast?" asked Marie.

"It's a trick I learned in the Legion. It is soda bread," Cameron wagged his finger from side to side, "no yeast."

"And you had everything you needed?"

"Yeah, sure. It is essentially just vinegar, water, flour, and baking soda, of course."

"Baking soude?"

"*Bicarbonate de soude.*"

"Marvelous," said Marie.

"Don't be so sure, though I guarantee it's better then pain de guerre, if you have ever had it. I wouldn't wish that on anyone."

"*Ce qui est du pain de guerre,* Mr. Kincaid?" asked Nicole.

"Pain de guerre, war bread, was something I ate a few times a day for the first few years of my hitch in the Legion. It's very nutritious," Cameron looked above the table, his face crumpled, "but hard as a rock and tastes," he moved his jaw around pretending to chew, "like paper mache might taste." He stuck his tongue out and curled his lips up. Cameron then smiled and broke off a piece of the soda bread. "Claude taught me how to make this. It's simple, but better."

"Hard as rock, how could you eat it?" Nicole shook her head.

"Well, the Legion is French. We got rations of wine and brandy when they were available. That helped."

CHAPTER 17
LAKE ONTARIO

After dinner, Nicole helped Marie clear the table then went up to the bedroom. Cameron put more wood in the hearth and then joined Marie in the kitchen.

"I have this. Mr. Kincaid. You already prepared such a fine meal."

"It's part of the process," said Cameron. He scraped what small amount of stew remained out of the tagine and into a smaller bowl. As the two cleaned the kitchen, they said nothing to each other. The music had stopped after they had sat down for dinner, but not until now did the cabin seem quiet. Cameron flipped the cassette tape and pressed play. "He has such a beautiful voice," said Marie.

"It's not electric guitar, that's for sure."

Marie nodded her head in agreement. "It certainly is not."

When the counters were clean and all of the dishes were in the soapy water of the sink, the two stood side by side, Cameron washing and Marie drying. Both were relaxed, their hands busy, the music, softer now, accompanying their task. Marie held a plate with part of a towel and dried the edge with the rest, rotating the dish in her hand with each stroke. She turned away from the plate and gazed at Cameron standing next to her. Humming along with Pavarotti, he was so at peace in the kitchen.

"Mr. Kincaid."

"Cameron, Marie." He turned his head to her and arched an eye, "You can call me Cameron."

"Mr. Kincaid," said Marie again. He sighed and looked back down at a plate next to the sink. He put the dish into the hot water. "Yes," said Cameron.

"I only wanted to tell you…"

"Yes?"

"Well, you look so natural in the kitchen."

"Thank you, I think."

"I mean, you are — were — a soldier. Now you are a chef. How does that happen?"

"You mean, how did I learn to cook?"

"No," said Marie, "though your food is wonderful, I imagine that you are a different man now than you were as a legionnaire."

"That is probably true."

"So how does that happen?"

Cameron handed Marie the last plate to dry and pulled the stopper from the sink to let the water drain. He then picked up a towel he had left sitting on the counter and began to dry his hands. "How does that happen?" he said. "I have Claude to thank, I guess."

"He taught you to cook?" asked Marie. She set down the last plate, now dry, and hung the towel she had been using.

"Yes, but more than that." Cameron opened the door to Pepe's wine cave and grabbed the neck of a bottle near the door. "He did teach me to cook, but he also taught me balance." He held the bottle up to the light and then reached for the corkscrew.

"Balance is important. To be sure," said Marie.

"Yeah, well, it started simply enough." Cameron plunged the corkscrew into the bottle. "The rations we had in the Legion left a bit to be desired. They've gotten better over the last few years, but early in my hitch, they were far more lacking." Cameron uncorked the bottle and poured the dark wine into two clean glasses. "Claude is an elder legionnaire: *Les Anciens,* as we say." He offered a glass to Marie, "I guess now I am, too. Regardless, Claude served in the French Far East expeditionary corps, way back." Cameron leaned back on the counter. "Then, the ration kits were composed of German and American stocks, as well as local food. Claude and the other *Anciens* all told me how good us young fellas had it." Marie, too, leaned against the counter. Cameron held up his arm and gestured toward the main room and the large sofa. "Claude told me that the legionnaires occupied their time fighting the Viet Minh purely so that they wouldn't focus on their own cooks." Marie smiled at Cameron's jest and sat on the sofa. He sat next to her. The fire crackled in the hearth and illuminated the room. The moon had moved across the sky and now shone through a different set of windows.

Cameron continued, "I guess it was at that time that Claude learned to cook for himself. He had some training before the Legion and a natural skill. He became very popular with those around him for having the ability to turn the rations into something great."

"And he taught you this?"

"Not right away. He did not want much to do with me at first."

"What changed that?"

"I saved his life."

Marie curled her leg under her. She unfastened the tightly wrapped towel from her head and let her auburn hair fall in front of her face. Cameron continued his story with his eyes locked on her. The way she naturally ran her fingers through her hair was so innocent, wholesome, and pure. When Marie lifted her head back to him, her face glowed faintly in the firelight. Her eyes twinkled. "So you got his attention," said Marie.

"Yes, you could say that. He opened up and we became close." Cameron paused and then said, "His mentorship saved my life many times in return." He took a sip of wine. "Ultimately, it was he that convinced me to leave the Legion with him, to learn to cook professionally, and to partner in Le Dragon Vert, our restaurant in New York."

"You don't think you would have done that without him, became a chef, I mean?"

"I don't know. Claude said I had a *je ne sais quoi* that led to a charmed life."

"I can see that," said Marie.

"Really?"

"You are a very interesting man, Mr. Kincaid."

Marie's eyes were inviting and her lips full. Cameron leaned toward her. "I told you, call me Cameron." He placed his lips against hers and kissed her. Marie responded by reaching around his shoulders and pulling him closer. The kiss was long and the two embraced tightly. Then Marie pulled her head away, "Mr. Kincaid."

Cameron looked into her eyes. "Cameron," he said again.

"Mr. Kincaid," said Marie, slowly shaking her head to either side, "I cannot."

"I understand," said Cameron. He let his arms fall from her sides.

A clanging of metal came from outside of the cabin where the Chevy was parked. Cameron and Marie sat upright. The P226 had been left upstairs. Cameron took the stairs two at a time and secured the handgun from the bureau drawer in the bedroom he had chosen for his own. He released the safety, pulled the slide back to cock the handgun, and then went back downstairs. Marie was on the edge of the couch with her hands on the inside of her knees. Marie saw the handgun and started to speak. Cameron threw his finger up to his lips. There was another clang. Cameron took his finger from in front of his lips and pointed toward the huge windowed wall and the glass door within that opened on to the deck over looking the lake. He then walked his middle and index fingers in a semicircle. Marie nodded. Cameron pointed at Marie, spread his hand flat, and slowly pressed his palm down through the air.

Cameron lifted the P226 to a line of fire and turned the latch of the glass door. The door opened silently. A light breeze, cool from the lake, whisked past the side of his face. He placed a bare foot on the deck, testing the wood for sound. The boards did not creak.

The deck was cold on his bare feet.

Slowly Cameron made his way to the edge of the deck. He knew that when he turned the corner, whoever was at the other end of the cabin would have the advantage of seeing him in silhouette against the lake. He decided his only advantage would be surprise. Cameron counted to three and on three lunged around the corner, P226 ready to fire. He saw no one. Stars filled the sky above the trees, which hid all below them in shadow. In the moonlit yard between the trees and the cabin no form or shadow moved. At the back of the cabin, around the side that Cameron could not yet see, the disturbance to the stillness continued. His body cant and both arms fully bent, Cameron made quick measured steps to the next corner. Cameron counted to three again and then on three hurled himself around the corner into a ready firing position.

Cameron immediately saw the culprit. The masked bandit paid no attention to the man with the gun standing barefoot at the corner. Marie had taken the trash out of the kitchen, placed the refuse in the large plastic bin by the door, and had not fastened the lid of the bin with the snap-on handles. The smell of the food scraps from the unsealed bin had lured a plump raccoon from the tree line.

Cameron straightened his legs and let the P226 rest by his side.

CHAPTER 18
LAKE ONTARIO

The aroma of fresh brewed coffee and the soft sounds of Mozart flowed to Cameron's bedside from the great room below. Cameron was quick to his feet, relaxed and refreshed. He had been barely a moment between the soft mattress and duvet before falling deep into sleep. If he dreamt, the dreams were fleeting. His only sense had been that his breath was heavy.

Cameron slipped on his pants and shirt, stepped out the balcony in front of his bedroom, rested both hands on the rail, and looked out onto the lake. Lake Ontario's dark waters from the night before were now cool blue and the far-off horizon cut a fine line below a peach ribbon of morning light. Below Cameron saw Nicole poking at the fire. Orange embers burst and snapped around the small logs in the hearth with each jab of the iron rod. Holding a cup of coffee Marie walked to the large windowed wall from the kitchen beneath the balcony to admire the morning light on the lake.

Marie sipped from her coffee and walked to Nicole. Above Nicole, Marie noticed Cameron on the balcony.

"Good morning," said Marie.

Nicole, still crouched before the fire, lifted her head up, "Good Morning Mr. Kincaid."

"Good Morning," said Cameron. He reached up and ran his fingers through his mussed hair, loosely scratching his scalp. He was glad to see the women in good spirits. Toronto, and what the visit to the city would mean for them, moved to the front of his mind.

CHAPTER 19
TORONTO

Back on the main highway, there was silence between them. Cameron tilted his head back and then side-to-side. The fingertips of one hand tap, tap, tapped the vinyl on the door and the fingertips of the other rested on the steering wheel. His eyes shifted from the road to the rearview mirror. Nicole was moving across the bench seat from the center to the passenger side window.

"It's strange," said Nicole.

"What is?" asked Marie.

"That sign."

Marie did not lift her head. The contents of her bag were spread on her lap and she was arranging and rearranging the items.

The sign that the Chevy was about to pass was a memorial highway marker. Two Edwardian crown–capped shields, similar to the single-shield signs they'd passed every few minutes as they traveled down the Lake Ontario coast, bordered the highway's name on a field of blue. One shield was numbered 401, marking the road as a Canadian highway, and the other displayed a poppy in place of a number. Between the two shields were the words "Highway of Heroes."

"I read about this memorial," said Cameron. "This strip of road is dedicated to Canada's fallen soldiers. The soldiers come into the country back at the Trenton military base and then the bodies are convoyed with family members to the coroner's office in Toronto."

"Always this way?"

"It started as a phenomenon, I guess. Crowds of patriotic Canadians were lining the overpasses to pay tribute to the soldiers and then it became kind of official."

"I understand," said Nicole. "That sounds very nice." The sign behind them, she found something else of interest. She moved back to the center of the seat to get a clearer look out the windshield, leaned forward, and rested her head between Cameron and Marie.

"What is that tower?"

"That is the CN tower," said Cameron, "a national landmark."

"CN?"

"Canadian National Tower."

The spire on the horizon dwarfed the Toronto skyline. The revolving restaurant brilliantly reflected the late afternoon sun and intermittently flared as they drew closer to the city.

"Is that where we are going?" asked Nicole.

Cameron looked over at Marie. He did not have an exact destination in mind, simply Toronto. Though Marie had begun to trust Cameron and was no longer overtly secretive, in the midst of their chaotic travel some things were still unfolding on a need-to-know basis. This did not bother Cameron and he was not put off when Marie returned his glance with a nod and answered Nicole with a yes.

"Will we be going up into the tower?"

"Yes, we will," said Marie.

"Hmm," said Nicole. She sat back in her seat, crossed her arms, and turned her head toward the lake.

* * * * *

The way to the tower was well marked. Without much effort, the three soon found themselves in a designated parking lot in its shadow. Cameron switched off the engine. After listening to the Chevy engine's numbing roar and the vibration of the tires on the highway, the silence was eerie. He stretched his arms far in front of him, interlocking his fingers. "So," said Cameron, adjusting the rearview mirror to see his own reflection. His hand ran over his forehead and his fingers through his hair. "What's next? I suppose we go in."

"Yes, Mr. Kincaid," said Marie. "We will meet someone here."

"The Perfect? Here?"

"No, that would be too easy. There is someone here who will direct us though."

"Ah, a contact."

"Yes, a contact. They are waiting for us."

Cameron shrugged and opened the car door. He took the idea of meeting a contact in stride. There had already been two rendezvous and two attempts on their lives. Cameron pulled back the release of the P226, inspected the handgun, and then stepped out of the car.

The three stretched when free from the Chevy. The rest at the cabin had not been enough to fully recover from the traveling of the last few days and the morning ride added to the toll.

They made their way to the base of the tower to wait for the elevator that would take them to the restaurant. A ticket booth stood at the end of a vacant velvet-roped lane. A small red sign next to the booth read "30 minutes from here."

"What is thirty minutes from here?" asked Nicole.

"Since there is nobody else waiting, it doesn't mean anything. If there was a line, it would take that long to get inside," said Cameron.

"No line — do you think they are open?"

"We're about to find out."

Cameron thought the booth was empty. He stepped up to the window and found a stocky Indian woman with thick glasses and a tight ponytail sitting on a stool behind the short counter. The woman's back was flat against the wall and she was staring intently into a paperback held a short distance from her face. The novel was titled "*The Potter's Daughter*" and there was a picture of a woman standing beneath a willow tree on the cover. The story must have been good because the woman did not notice Cameron until he tapped the window and even then, she did not look away from the book. She simply said, "How many?" in a tone that indicated that her mind was somewhere other than in the small white shed where she sat.

"Three for the restaurant," said Cameron.

Without looking up, she lifted her hand above her head to a computer terminal on the counter, and tapped the keyboard three times. "Sixty-nine dollars please."

"Just to get to the restaurant?"

She sighed, tilted her head to the terminal screen, and then slid her glasses up the bridge of her nose.

"Three for the sky pod is twenty-five fifty. The tickets can be used toward the price of your meal."

Cameron gave her the money in exchange for three passes. The woman went back to her book and gave no further acknowledgment when he wished her a good day. Cameron rolled his eyes and turned back to Marie and Nicole. He extended his arm down the velvet-roped path toward the elevators. "Right this way," said Cameron.

They entered a glass-fronted atrium housing six elevator bays. One set of elevator doors was already open. A squat older man sat near the door on a short, pillowed stool. He took the passes Cameron handed him, scanned them with an optical reader, and then handed them back. "Step to the back please," said the man. The three did as the older man requested and stepped to the back wall of the elevator. Next to the man was a metal panel with a key in the lock. The man grasped the key and gave his hand a quick turn, opened the panel, and then flipped a switch that caused the elevator doors to shut behind them. "Hold on," said the man and then he turned a knob above the door switch. A light in the panel flashed green and the floor started to rise, pushing at their feet with a soft sudden thrust. The horizon filled the glass wall and below them two large glass panels in the floor of the elevator looked down on the shaft that, at the speed they were lifting, fell away beneath them.

"Whoa," said Nicole.

"This is the fastest elevator in North America," said the squat man. "You'll never ride anything like it."

"I should say not," said Marie.

The glass carriage brought a literal levity to their day. Over the next minute the horizon dropped below them and the buildings of the Toronto skyline, the parts they could see, shrunk to miniatures.

The elevator slowed to a stop. "Welcome to the Sky Pod. See you after your meal." The squat man smiled and opened the doors.

CHAPTER 20
TORONTO

The three entered the restaurant through a small wood-paneled lobby. Dark walnut furnishings accented the room and glass walls slanted out over the city and the lake far below.

The maître d' stood behind a computer-topped podium. He greeted them and tapped an image of the seating plan on the computer display. A virtual table lit green. He looked up at the three, smiled, and directed them toward the corresponding table at the edge of the room.

Marie and Nicole, fascinated with the view, were drawn to the huge windows. Cameron looked to the interior. He had heard of the infamous wine cellar, the world's highest. Through double cherry doors, Cameron could see redwood racks stocked with bottle after bottle of wine.

"Incredible," said Marie, gazing to the shore far across the lake.

"It certainly is," said Cameron, still looking at the wine cellar.

Cameron, Marie, and Nicole each took a seat at their window-side table and the maître d' placed menus in front of them. A waiter sidled up to him and then stepped to the table as the maître d' stepped away.

"Hello," said the waiter, "my name is Christophe. Would you like sparkling water today?"

"That would be fine," said Cameron.

"May I tell you the specials we have today?"

"I believe we know what we will be ordering," said Marie.

Cameron had not yet opened his menu. He looked across the table to Marie. Her eyes were fixed on the waiter's. "I understand that you have swan, white swan. We would like that."

The waiter's smile fell away and his brow dropped. He quickly scanned Marie, Cameron, and then Nicole. Nicole was lost in her gaze across the lake and indifferent to the waiter's presence. If the waiter was trying to be nonchalant in his reaction, he failed. He fixed his eyes back onto Marie and then composed himself. His smile returned, tightened and hubristic, "Excellent choice, *madame.*" Marie handed the waiter her and Nicole's menus, as did Cameron. "I will alert the chef," said the waiter, he nodded, and then went to the kitchen.

Cameron turned to the window and tilted his head to the side, "I have to say, that was efficient. I have never had white swan."

"Nor will you, Mr. Kincaid. The white swan has long been a symbol of the Cathar. They have been waiting for us."

"They? You mean they are Cathar as well?"

"In a matter of speaking. There have always been those that help us. The believers who adhere to the Cathar ideal but are not austere. They do not aspire to become Perfects."

"Like laymen?"

"We have no hierarchy as such. The austere Cathar are Perfects and all other believers are Credentes. The dedications of the believers range from follower and supporter of the traditions to that of austerity. Nicole and I are Credentes."

"Perfects and Credentes."

Not shifting her view from the water, Nicole spoke. "Not everyone that has accepted the true belief is prepared to separate from this world. For some it takes many lives. They are still *bon gens.*"

"Good people."

"Yes, the good people, the pure ones and those that strive to be pure. The followers of the true faith."

"And women, they can be either Credentes or Perfects?"

"The *bon gens* have always believed in female equality. It is yet another reason for the Rex Mundi to despise us. All souls are equal, and through their reoccurring physical manifestations may take the form of either man or woman."

"That does not sound like equality to me," said Cameron.

"How so?"

"I just heard you say that women are treated equally perchance they were men in their last lives. That does not sound like real equality."

"That is not how we see it. We see souls without gender, equal regardless of their previous manifestations. We were the first to believe that the New Testament was for everyone, not only the church."

"I bet that went over well, too."

Cameron did not need to see past the swinging doors into the kitchen to know there was a disturbance. The commotion was audible. Raised whispers over raised whispers escalated. The excitement of the kitchen staff caught the attention of the maître d', who was strolling beside a row of window tables. Cameron saw him turn toward the kitchen, brow down, mouth agape, and hands spread away from his chest. He was in an exchange with someone out of Cameron's view. The maître d's eyes went tight and he stepped fast into the kitchen. The whispers died down and then the maître d' slid his head into view.

He peered at the table, said something Cameron could not make out, and then moved back to the kitchen.

"Well. You have their attention," said Cameron.

"As we should," said Marie.

CHAPTER 21
TORONTO

Christophe came out of the kitchen a moment later carrying a large tray, his chin high and eyes set forward in the stance of a professional. The maître d' trailed behind Christophe, his posture as disciplined as the waiter's. The gold foil of a champagne bottle poked out of the silver bucket tucked under the maître d's arm. Their march as uniformed as any soldier's, the maître d' and Christophe made a sharp right-angle turn toward the table. A tall, lean busboy scurried out of the kitchen carrying a stand for the bucket in one hand and a stand for the tray in the other and maneuvered around them to get to the table first. The dance could not have been choreographed any better. The bus boy set up the stands, and just as swiftly, Christophe and the maître d' wove around him, resting the platter and bucket, then setting to work immediately. "*Monsieur, madame, madame,*" said the maître d'. He had not spoken when seating them and now the words rushed from his mouth, "I am sure that you will find this bottle to your liking." He held the champagne above the table, turned from the table to the platter, and picked up a large knife. Cameron had performed this trick many times himself and knew what was coming next. The maître d' lifted the knife high above the neck of the bottle and then brought the blade down onto the cork with a pop, releasing a small spout of bubbly foam. Christophe placed four small plates of food on the table, two in each hand, and then produced three flutes from the tray. As each flute was placed in front of one of the restaurant's special guests, the maître d' filled it with champagne.

Marie and Nicole held hands and recited the Lord's Prayer. Cameron smiled across the table at Marie when the prayer was finished and she returned the smile in her eyes.

Christophe placed four more small plates onto the quickly crowding table and the busboy leaned over Cameron's other shoulder to fill the water glasses.

"Today you will be having an assortment of tastes from our kitchen. I am sure you will find them appropriate and to your liking." Christophe gestured to each of the plates and began to list off the delicacies that occupied them. "Here you will find morels stuffed with garlic and almond, olives anchova, pesto rosso made with sun-dried tomatoes and bell pepper — no cheese in this," Christophe winked after he added that necessary qualifier. He then went to the next plate, "Wild mushroom, morel again, and asparagus ravioli, also no cheese, zucchini carpaccio, crispy eggplant with tomatoes and basil, baby artichokes in a black truffle sauce, and lastly, chanterelle mushrooms on wheat berry risotto with sage leaves."

Christophe stood straight and placed his hands together in front of him.

"The presentation is excellent," said Cameron, "very... Provençal."

"Very good, *monsieur*," said Christophe, then closed his eyes and bowed his head.

Christophe then glanced down at Marie. Cameron could tell that Christophe was obviously waiting for a comment. Marie placed both of her hands flat on the table, looked across to Cameron, and then surveyed the foods Christophe had presented.

Christophe drew his next few words slowly. "Our apologies. *Madame*, perhaps we have offered too many mushroom dishes?"

Languidly Marie turned her head up toward Christophe, his opened mouth smile turning to an inviting gape, his head beginning to droop. "Disappointing," said Marie. "Mushrooms in any form disagree with me." Christophe's head shot back up and his smile went full, "I am sure *madame* will find these mushrooms very much to her liking." The maître d' approached the table, slightly nudging Christophe for position, and produced a plate domed with a silver lid. "I think you will find these sweets to your liking as well," said the maître d'. He placed the plate on the table and bowed. Christophe and the busboy bowed as well. "*Bénisse, personne n'est content que nous,*" they said almost in unison. Marie and Nicole bowed their heads back at them and repeated the greeting. The maître d' then, along with the busboy, turned away from the table and headed back toward the kitchen. Christophe lifted his hands, still clasped together, to his chest. "If you need anything, let me know. The busboy will be bringing some bread shortly. We are baking it fresh for you."

"*Merçi,*" said Marie. "*Merçi,*" said Cameron and Nicole.

After Christophe left for the kitchen, Cameron put his hands on his lap. "This food looks marvelous," said Cameron. "Too bad about the mushrooms, the chanterelles are a delicacy."

Marie reached over to the stuffed mushrooms and picked one up, "Actually I prefer morels," she said, and then bit into the cap. "Yum, delicious."

"But I thought you said…"

Nicole interrupted, "She said what she was supposed to. Ordering the white swan was not enough."

"Oh," said Cameron.

Marie lifted the domed lid from the plate revealing an envelope pinned between small cakes. She took the envelope, broke the wax seal, and then lifted the flap to look inside. "The question was a secondary measure. The information in this envelope is quite precious. These gentlemen do not even know its contents."

"It is the location of the Perfect. Correct?"

"Yes. A new envelope is sent by messenger each week and the one from the week before is destroyed by fire in the presence of at least three."

Cameron put his fork into an olive, "And you know this because?" He put the olive into his mouth. Nicole answered, "Our security methods are old, simple, and efficient. This is the way this has been done for hundreds of years."

"But if somebody got a hold of the envelope, they would have the secret."

Marie handed the envelope across the table. "It would mean nothing to anyone other then those sending it and those for whom it is intended. Even our friends here would not know the meaning."

Cameron took the envelope and looked inside. On a small card was a blue outline of a dove. "And you know what this means?" asked Cameron.

"It means you will need a big appetite," said Marie.

CHAPTER 22
TORONTO

They arrived at their next destination soon after leaving the CN Tower. Though the distance was short enough to walk, Marie suggested they park the car a few blocks away. After finding a public lot near Trinity College, they walked over to Yonge Street.

They easily found the address they were looking for. Built some time near the beginning of the last century, the two-story building was sandwiched between two others from different eras, one more ancient, and the other no more than a decade old. Though Yonge Street was a long established Toronto artery, Cameron could see no main architectural theme. A few blocks toward the lake from where they stood, forty story buildings randomly shot up interspersed with two and three story buildings, an architectural potpourri. Cameron remembered reading somewhere that Yonge Street was the longest street in the world and wondered now if a lack of continuity shouldered the curbs the entire thousand-mile length.

When they got to the building Cameron understood why Marie quipped that he may need a big appetite. The remark had been an attempt at humor.

Across the first floor glass facade were the words "Thai Lotus Flower Restaurant" in tall saffron letters above and below a sizable disk of the same color. A lotus flower was stenciled within the disk, a simple Buddhist mandala Cameron recognized from his trips to the Far East.

The modern dining room was overdone in saffron. Geometric panels of coarse saffron fabric covered the saffron walls and cushioned benches of the same shade ran the full length of the room. Several dark wooden tables lined the benches and a few larger round tables ran through the center of the room. Large milky globes, giant upside-down lollipops thought Cameron, hung from the ceiling in two uniformed rows, bathing the room in an even ambient light.

At the back of the restaurant was a backlit acrylic wall with water cascading down its face. In front of the water wall a thin Thai Buddha statue sat cross-legged and open palmed, smiling softly at the room already busy with an early dinner crowd of tourists grabbing a bite on their way to or from one of the many musicals that played in the area.

"So how does a blue dove equate to a Thai restaurant?" asked Cameron.

"It was not a blue dove," said Marie, "it was a zebra dove."

Cameron smirked at Marie and Nicole added, "The zebra dove is native to Thailand."

"So you knew that symbol meant the Lotus Flower?"

"So we knew," said Marie.

Cameron pulled open the heavy glass door and gestured to Marie and Nicole to step inside. A warm vapor of ginger wafted past them through the door. A young thin Thai man with scruffy orange hair and a shiny blue silk suit greeted them with an open smile that lowered his jaw down to his collar. "I have this," said Cameron to Marie. He then said to the man, "*Swạsdī reā kả lạng mxng hā pheụ̀ xn.*"

The man's jaw came together and the corners of his mouth pulled back. "Listen fella," said the young man, "I barely speak the old language."

"Sorry," said Cameron, "I said that we were looking for a friend."

"A lot of people here tonight." The young man craned his head back behind him to view the entirety of the room, "Do you see your friend?"

Marie glanced at Cameron and then leaned to the man's ear. Though she whispered, Cameron could hear the two words clearly. They were "white swan."

The man's smile returned to an open jaw and he lifted his right hand to the side of his head to run his fingers through his already mussed hair. "Ah," said the young man, "I know your friend and I will take you to her. Follow me." He turned into the dining room and headed to the back of the room without turning back, taking long strides with his lean, limber body. The three exchanged satisfied glances and began to pursue the young man before he left them behind.

Large portions of noodles and rice filled each table they passed, offering aromas of basil, ginger, or the unmistakable tang that could only come from sweet chili sriracha, and when they entered the kitchen, those aromas grew substantially. New and clean with lots of stainless steel, the kitchen was an organized pandemonium of saffron-bloused wait staff along one side and a line of scurrying cooks along the other. Large bright white ceramic tiles covering the walls echoed back all of the clanging and chirping of the busy hour. Nicole ducked her head below the many pans hanging above a center counter to see what she could of the gas stove tops shooting flames against the far wall and the three short Thai cooks who each appeared to have three to four arms at the speed which they were moving.

Halfway through the kitchen, the orange-haired man slipped around the end of a stainless counter that hugged the wall and pushed a tall stainless-steel metro rack forward to reveal a pocket door. He then slid open the pocket door and disappeared into the wall. The three followed him inside to a small room. To the right was a stack of empty crates and large bags of onions and rice, to the left another metro rack filled with dozens of plastic containers full of dried spice. The orange-haired man pulled the spice-covered rack away from the wall revealing yet another pocket door. Behind this door was a stairwell that led back toward the front of the building, lit only by a small window at the top of the stairs. Close behind each other, Cameron, Marie, and Nicole squeezed through the space between the metro rack and the doorframe and climbed the creaky wooden steps.

Standing below the small circular window on the top landing, the young man's orange hair looked dirty brown and his blue suit no longer had sheen. Without the flamboyant props and animated smile Cameron saw the young man for what he was, a boy in his late teens.

The young man rapped on a metal door in a broken rhythm, waited a second, and then repeated. The door opened as Nicole reached the landing. At the top of the door, a thin brass security chain kept it from opening more than a few inches. Near the bottom of the door, Cameron could see a heavy steel chain was also in place. The young man rattled off something in Thai that sounded to Cameron, loosely translated, like "they have arrived." Cameron turned to Marie and Nicole and grinned. The young man had developed a sudden recollection of the old language.

Through the door, they saw first a man's forehead and then an eye briefly peek around the edge of the door. The door then shut with a thud. They could hear the sound of the security chain being unfastened from the door and the heavy chain below falling to the floor with a clank. Then the door opened again, this time wide.

CHAPTER 23
TORONTO

An old balding Thai man with thick glasses stood in the doorway. He wore a sweater buttoned over a white-collar shirt that was closed all the way to the top and his black slacks fit loosely. The old man reminded Cameron of someone's grandfather.

"Come in, come in," said the old man. Cameron was surprised by the man's deep froggy voice and unmistakable British accent.

The young man turned away from the door. "There you go," said the young man, punctuated with another of his open-mouthed smiles. He slid by Cameron and the women back down the stairs.

The older man stepped back from the door, "Welcome, I am Ananda."

"Hello, my name is Cameron."

Cameron stepped through the door. He held his hand out to the old man only to have his wrist grabbed by Marie. Cameron flashed Marie a glance and she subtly shook her head. Cameron lowered his arm and proceeded to introduce Marie and Nicole. "Ananda," said Cameron, "this is —."

"—Miss Marie and Miss Nicole," interrupted Ananda.

"*Bénisse, personne n'est content que nous,*" the women said almost in unison with their heads bowed. Ananda returned the greeting.

Something occurred to Cameron. Neither of the women had met Ananda before, yet he knew them by name. Ananda had been waiting for them after all and was sincerely pleased to see them.

Faded pink floral wallpaper covered the walls and white panel curtains muted the daylight, making the room hazy and ethereal. The only furniture in the room was an old sofa that sat between an empty coffee table and the windows and, against the far wall, an old, round, tapestry covered table. On the table were a small Buddha statue much like the one in the restaurant below and a short lamp with an embroidered shade and red tassels. The French doors centered on the interior wall were draped and closed.

Ananda shut the door and refastened the security chain. Cameron could now see, though the upper chain was as any he had seen before, the ends of the heavy bottom chain were permanently anchored into the floor to ensure no one was able to get through the door while the chain was fastened. The length of the chain was threaded through three thick eyebolts screwed into the bottom of the door, fastening the door to the apartment. If the hinges were ever broken, the door would still be chained to the floor. Ananda pulled the slack of the chain tight and slipped a thick padlock through the doubled-up links. The door could not be opened without unlocking the padlock. Ananda turned the key in the padlock, then removed and slipped the key into his pocket when he stood. Ananda then turned back to his three visitors and smiled. "Are you hungry? Would you like some tea?" asked Ananda, adding quickly before any had a chance to reply, "I only have tea here, but I can call downstairs for anything you like."

"*Merçi,* that is very generous," said Marie. "We ate."

"But of course you did," said Ananda. "I understand

the food at the tower is very good." He winked at Nicole and she smiled in return. "Probably just as well that we do not dawdle." His eyes focused on something in front of them that could not be seen. "She has been asking for you. It is not long now." Ananda hung his head for a short moment. When Ananda lifted his head, again his pleasant demeanor returned. "But that is why you have been sent for." Nicole offered her arms to the old grandfather. "No," said Ananda, "I may no longer feel the touch of a woman." He closed his eyes tightly. "I feel your compassion though."

Nicole closed her eyes tightly for a moment and then said, "*Parcite Nobis.* For all the sins, I have ever done in thought, word, and deed. I ask pardon of God, of the Church, and of you. Bless me, Lord and pray for me. Lead us to our rightful end."

"God bless you. In our prayers, we ask from God to make a good Christian out of you and lead you to your rightful end. So you are blessed. Are you now ready, young Nicole?"

"This is the life I have chosen," said Nicole.

Cameron did not realize at that time the significance of Nicole's answer and would later think back on the words.

"Very good, then," Ananda raised his eyes to the others, "she will want to see all of you. Come this way."

Ananda pulled another key from his pocket to unlock the French doors. He pulled them open, one in each hand, revealing a small kitchen. They walked through another set of open French doors behind the kitchen then passed through a sitting room that held three cushioned chairs and another small, round, tapestry covered table, this one with an old television sitting on top with rabbit ear antennas. Cameron thought the television was too old to be color and was not surprised that the cord dangling behind the table was unplugged.

The next room was lit by the daylight of an adjacent room, which streamed through yet another set of French doors. Ananda stopped short in front of these doors, one of which was opened slightly. "I will tell her you are here," said Ananda and then slipped into the room. He had barely started to shut the door behind him when the three heard a warm and musical voice exclaim, "Just bring them in here."

The door swung open and Ananda shuffled the three into a large bedroom.

"May I present Lady Mani and Lady Yada?"

Thin translucent curtains billowed on the far wall, barely masking the red wooden deck and the leafy top branches of the maple tree in the courtyard. The only furniture in the room was a bed, a small wooden chair, and a cot on the opposite wall. On the bed, a Thai woman sat upright on the pillows, covered to her waist by a pink blanket the hue of the pink lotus flowers sprouting from bright leafy green stems on the large watercolor above the bed. Lady Mani's long silver hair cascaded down her shoulders over her cotton gown. Her vibrant almond eyes and warm toothy smile gave the old woman a young, giddy, sprightly appearance. On the chair next to the bed sat Lady Yada, another silver-haired woman though younger more reserved than Lady Mani, even in her smile.

Marie and Nicole dropped to their knees, bowed three times, and then chimed, "*Parcite Nobis.* For all the sins, I have ever done in thought, word, and deed. I ask pardon of God, of the Church, and of you. Bless me, Lord, and pray for me. Lead us to our rightful end."

Lady Mani responded to the two women warmly, "God bless you. In our prayers, we ask from God to make good Christians out of you and lead you to your rightful end."

"Come here, the three of you," said Lady Mani. "Unfortunately I am not moving too well."

"She has all but begun the endura," said Ananda.

"She has been waiting for you," said Lady Yada.

Lady Mani sensed that Cameron did not know what "endura" meant. "That means, young man, that I will soon stop eating and drinking so that the end may come and I can return to heaven and let this life be my last. That is the endura."

"I'm not sure I understand," said Cameron.

Nicole took his hand, "Ananda and Lady Mani are *Parfaits*, Perfects. They have lived many lives but the lives they live now are their last in this realm. When they leave the these physical forms, they will leave the evil and temptation of Rex Mundi and the world he has created."

"So you will let yourself die?"

"Oh, I am dying, young one. There is no reason to slow it now. No worries to have, I would soon fast for forty days regardless. My purpose is almost complete."

Lady Yada smiled at Lady Mani.

"And Lady Yada, is she a Perfect too?"

"It is my honor to assist the Perfect," said Lady Yada.

"As it will be mine," said Marie.

Nicole squeezed Cameron's hand and then walked over to the edge of the bed.

"Are you ready, child?" asked Lady Mani.

"I have prepared myself, *Parfaite*."

"I am sure you have little one. I myself accepted this gift when I was a bit younger than you. I knew then that this was to be my last life. I also thought I knew the responsibility that this gift would put upon me. I only now know the full truth of this gift."

"I should wish to be wise enough to learn the truth and will do my best to uphold the responsibility, *Parfaite*."

"I believe you will, Nicole, as others have for generations." Lady Mani looked up at Marie and Cameron. "I would like you to stay for the consolamentum as witnesses. Besides," she gazed directly to Marie, "learning of our ways will help this young man through this life. Answer his questions. He will have many."

"Yes, of course, *Parfaite*," said Marie.

CHAPTER 24
CONSOLAMENTUM ONE

Nicole knelt away from Lady Mani as Lady Yada eased the old woman to the edge of the bed. Lady Mani moved her weak, thin legs from under the blanket and over the side of the bed, and then, with no small effort, pulled herself up between the headboard and Lady Yada until she stood against the wall. Lady Mani then turned toward Nicole and smiled.

Cameron whispered to Marie, "May I ask, what is the consolamentum?"

Lady Mani looked at Marie, "Tell him, dear. The young knight deserves to know."

Marie answered Cameron in a soft voice, "The consolamentum is our sacrament, the only sacrament of the Cathari. It is a baptism of the Holy Spirit, a baptismal regeneration, absolution, and ordination all in one. When one receives the sacrament, they become a Perfect."

"Ordination, like a priest?"

"It is more than that. It is important to understand that our beliefs are based on the idea that love and power are incompatible. The physical is a manifestation of power, so the physical is incompatible with love. We are what has come to be called dualist. We believe in two Gods, evil and good, equal and comparable in status in heaven. The physical world is evil, created by Rex Mundi, the God of the Old Testament. He is all that is corporeal, chaotic, and powerful. The God of the New Testament that we worship is disincarnate. The good God is of pure spirit and completely untainted by matter. He is the God of love, order, and peace. The world has been tricked that the two are the same."

"They are different, then?" asked Cameron.

"When Rex Mundi created the physical world, he trapped pure human spirits and brought them into the corruption of the physical body and world. Death merely causes the soul to transfer to another body, either human or animal," said Marie.

"Reincarnation," said Cameron.

"One can only attain salvation by breaking the cycle of rebirth in the physical realm. This is why Jesus, the son of the good God, was sent to earth, to show man the way to salvation. Jesus performed the consolamentum on his disciples and they in turn performed the rite on others, placing their hands on those receiving the sacrament and saying a prayer. What you are watching is the literal transference of the holy spirit from Lady Mani to Nicole, as the holy spirit, descended from heaven, has been transferred by touch all the way back to Jesus."

"All the way back to Jesus?" asked Cameron.

"An unbroken line of salvation. In 2 Corinthians 4:4, the New Testament says 'the God of this world has blinded the minds of unbelievers, so that they cannot see the light of the gospel of the glory of Christ.' Our Lord Jesus was discarnate like his father. Jesus was a life-giving spirit that only appeared human," said Marie.

"He wasn't?"

"No. This sacrament is very special. The purpose of man's life on earth is to transcend matter, perpetually renouncing anything connected with the Rex Mundi, and attaining union with the God of love. This is Nicole's transition from Credentes to Perfect. There are only two ways to become a Perfect. To be deemed worthy after a long period of preparation and instruction as Nicole, or as a request on the deathbed."

"Like last rites?"

"Very much. The last rites of the Catholic Church are modeled after the Consolamentum. With the sacrament Nicole will gain true salvation and the ability to lead others to salvation."

Lady Mani took a black book, old yet not tattered, from next to her pillow and raised the tome in both hands above Nicole's head. Though there was no writing that Cameron could see, he believed the book to be a Bible. Lady Mani began to speak in Latin, "*Benedicite, Benedicite, Domine Deus, Pater bonorum spirituum, adjuva nos in ommibus quae facere voluerimus.*"

Cameron did not understand the blessing and wondered if the whole ceremony would be in Latin. Lady Mani then began to recite the Lord's Prayer in English.

Cameron caught himself mouthing the words.

Lady Mani continued, "You are the Temple of the Living God, as God has said, 'I dwell in them and walk in them, and I will be their God and they shall be my people. Touch not the unclean thing and I will receive you, and if you love me, keep my commandments. I will abide with you forever, the Spirit of Truth, whom the world cannot receive because the world cannot see or know me. You know me, for I dwell with you, and shall be in you. I am with you always, even unto the end of the world. Know that you are the temple of God, and that the Spirit of God dwells in you. If any man defiles the temple of God, I shall destroy him, for the Temple of God is holy, and you are a temple. For it is not you that speaks but the Spirit of God that speaks in you.' By this we know that we abide in Him and He in us, for He has given us His Spirit."

Marie whispered to Cameron, "She is explaining that the Holy Spirit is to be transferred to Nicole as according to scripture."

Lady Mani looked down at Nicole, "You are here in the place where Father, Son, and Holy Ghost have their spiritual abode, to receive that Holy Prayer which the Lord Jesus gave to his disciples."

"Like a six-degree separation from Jesus Christ," said Cameron.

"There are many more than six, and Nicole has studied to learn them all. But yes, she continues the unbroken line of the sacrament."

Lady Mani's voice became soothing, "You must learn that if you would receive this Holy Prayer you must repent your sins and forgive all men. For Our Lord Jesus Christ says, 'If you forgive not men their trespasses, neither will your Heavenly Father forgive your trespasses.' Hence it is meet and right that you be resolved in your heart to keep this Holy Prayer all your life according to the custom of the Church of God, in purity and truth, and in all other virtues which God would bestow upon you. Wherefore we pray the good Lord who bestowed upon the disciples of Jesus Christ the virtue to receive this Holy Prayer steadfastly that he may grant to you also the grace to receive it steadfastly, in his honor and for your salvation."

Lady Mani then began again recite the Lord's Prayer and Nicole followed her, line for line. Then of the prayer Lady Mani said, "We deliver you this Holy Prayer that you may receive it of us and of God and of the Church, that you may have the power to say it all your life, day and night, alone or in company, and that you must never eat or drink without first saying it." With a matter of fact tone Lady Mani added, "If you omit to do so you must do penance."

Nicole replied, "I receive it of you and of the Church." Then Nicole bowed at Lady Mani's feet.

"She is giving thanks, the melhoramentum," said Marie.

Lady Mani then three times asked Nicole, "My sister, do you desire to give yourself to our faith?" and three times Nicole answered, "yes," each time bowing and advancing one step. Between each step Nicole said, "Bless me." To each Lady Mani replied, "God bless and keep you." The third time bowing Nicole added, "Lord, pray to God for me, a sinner, that He will lead me to the good end." Lady Mani's response modified accordingly, "God bless you and make you a good Christian and bring you to the good end. Do you give yourself to God and the Gospel?"

"Yes," said Nicole.

"Do you promise that henceforth you will eat neither meat nor eggs, nor cheese, nor fat, that you live only from water and wood?"

"Water and wood?" asked Cameron. Marie answered, "Fish and vegetables." He nodded his head.

Lady Mani continued, "that you will not lie, that you will not swear, that you will not kill, that you will not abandon your body to any form of luxury?" Nicole's eyes were now tearing at Lady Mani's soothing litany, "that you will never go alone when it is possible to have a companion, that you will never sleep without breeches and shirt and that you will never abandon your faith for fear of water, fire, or any other manner of death?"

"Yes," said Nicole.

"You wish to receive the spiritual baptism whereby the Holy Spirit is given in the Church of God with the Holy Prayer by the laying on of hands of the Good Men."

"Yes," said Nicole.

"And lo, I am with you always, even unto the end of the world. Jesus Christ instituted this gift of the Holy Spirit by the laying on of hands."

"The actual consoling happens now," said Marie.

CHAPTER 25
CONSOLAMENTUM TWO

Lady Mani laid her hands on Nicole so that Nicole could receive the Holy Spirit.

Then looking upward, Lady Mani said, "This Holy Baptism by which the Holy Spirit is given to the Church of God has come from the Good Men to the Good Men and shall until the end of the world. As my Father has sent me, so send I you. As when he breathed on them and said unto them 'Receive Ye the Holy Ghost,' whatsoever sins you remit they are remitted unto them, and whatsoever sins you regain, they are regained."

Marie leaned over to Cameron again, "That means if she sins, loses austerity in the slightest, all of those she has blessed will have lost their blessing."

"If you wish to receive this power you must know that he has commanded that you shall not commit adultery or murder or lie, that you must not swear any oath, that you shall not seize or rob, nor do to others what you would not have done to yourself. That you must forgive whoever wrongs you and love your enemies, pray for your detractors and accusers, and bless them. If anyone strikes you on one cheek, turn to him the other also, and if anyone takes away your cloak, to leave him your coat also, and that you should neither judge nor condemn."

"Also you must hate this world and its works and the things of the world, love not the world or the things that are in the world. If any man loves the world, the love of the Father is not in him. For all that is in the world, the lust of the flesh and the lust of the eyes and the pride of life, is not of God but is of the world. The world will pass away, but he that does the will of God abides forever."

Cameron looked to Marie for clarification. "The material world is a lie of the evil Rex Mundi," said Marie.

Lady Mani shifted her eyes to Nicole's, "And Christ said, 'The world cannot hate you, but me it hates because I bear witness of it that its works are evil. I have seen all the works that are done under the sun, and behold, all is vanity and vexation of Spirit. Hate the solid garment of flesh.' By these witnesses, you must keep the commandments of God and hate the world, and if you continue well to the end, we have the hope that your soul shall have life eternal."

"I have this will," said Nicole, "pray to God for me that he will give me his power."

Marie took her cue and with Ananda and Lady Yada said, "*Parcite Nobis*. Good Christian, we pray you by the love of God that you grant this blessing, which God had given you, to our friend here present."

Nicole then said, "*Parcite Nobis*. For all the sins, I have ever done in thought, word, and deed. I ask pardon of God, of the Church, and of you all."

Then Marie, Ananda, Lady Yada, and Lady Mani replied, "By God and by us and by the Church, may your sins be forgiven and we pray God to forgive you them. *Adoremus, Patrem et Filium et Spiritum Sanctam.*"

Ananda walked over beside Nicole, Lady Yada, and Lady Mani. The four once again recited the Lord's Prayer followed by a passage from the Bible. Cameron knew the verse at once as he had heard the lines so many times in his youth. The passage was from the book of John, "In the beginning was the Word, and the Word was with God, and the Word was God."

Though he recognized the words of the first and following passages of the book of John, they now were shadowed with the beliefs of those around him. Particularly the last line they recited, "For the law was given by Moses, grace and truth came by Jesus Christ." Truth came by way of Jesus, thought Cameron — at least what they interpreted to be the truth.

Cameron absorbed Marie's words and listened to the final prayers for peace that Lady Mani spoke aloud to Nicole. He tried to comprehend how the weight of being a Perfect would bear on Nicole for the rest of her life. He could understand the idea of living an austere life, such as a nun or a monk. To fully comprehend what this would mean in their faith was something else.

Cameron did not have long to think. Below the apartment, people began to yell. There were gunshots and then more yelling. The commotion from the first floor restaurant reflected in the faces of everyone in the room.

Ananda's jaw slacked and he turned toward Cameron, unsure of his next action, "It is the worst. They are here."

CHAPTER 26
TORONTO

Ananda slowly reached into his pocket and then offered his hand to Cameron. In Ananda's hand, Cameron saw the dull brass key for the padlock on the bottom of the door.

From downstairs, they could hear screams and more gunfire. Cameron looked at the key and then into Ananda's lost eyes. "I'm sorry, sir, I don't think we'll be leaving that way." He then raised his voice to the women, "Marie, Nicole, help Lady Yada get Lady Mani dressed and gather up whatever they need. I am going to try to buy us some time."

Nicole embraced Lady Mani. The old woman no longer showed the strength that had emanated from her only moments ago when she performed the consolamentum. Now her vibrant eyes became childlike and her frail body began to shrink. Lady Yada put her arm around Lady Mani. "Here, child, let's help her to the bed," said Lady Yada.

The gunshots had stopped and now the only yelling came from two urgent and authoritative voices. Cameron's commando training kicked in. The muffled words coming from the yelling voices did not matter. The tone told Cameron what he wanted to know. Someone was being interrogated in the kitchen while the other voice barked out orders. The picture came clear to Cameron. He calculated at least four armed and disciplined individuals were running around downstairs and they would soon figure out that the people they were looking for were on the second floor.

Marie turned to Cameron, "Please hurry." She still sounded somewhat calm.

"You won't even know I'm gone," said Cameron.

Cameron made his way back toward the front of the apartment. He reached under his shirt and pulled the P226 from between his belt and lower back. Though he did not think anyone could hear him below, he stepped as lightly as he could.

Cameron stopped short of the door and froze. He listened to see if the gunmen downstairs had found their way into the small hidden room and the adjoining stairwell. The pocket doors were not that well hidden and there were many implements in the kitchen that could be used to make someone talk.

Cameron inspected the padlock and chain again and then the room. The chain-reinforced metal door made the entry as secure as possible without rebuilding the whole wall. The only way that anyone was getting through the door was to push through the entire doorframe and, from the sound of the assault, Cameron bet the men downstairs would figure that out sooner than later. No doubt, the men would have explosives. Barricading the door with the sofa could be enough of a deterrent to buy some time.

Cameron went over to the sofa and attempted to drag the heavy piece of furniture over to the door by lifting the end. The large sofa did not budge. On closer inspection, he realized the heavy sofa was a sofa bed. That would make sense — he had not seen a bed for Ananda and was pretty sure that the cot in the bedroom was Lady Yada's. The heavier the better. Cameron had to quickly find a way to get the oversized sofa away from the window to the front of the door.

As an elite legionnaire, Cameron was required to use his mind and his body. Sometimes brawn was all that was necessary. He went over to the far end of the sofa and set his P226 on the floor. Cameron lay on his back, contracting his body tightly to fit in the space between the sofa and the wall. His feet pressed firmly on the wall and his shoulders up against the sofa, Cameron pushed his legs and shoulders away from each other with all of his force. His muscles tensed, bulged, and turned to tight bricks. He could feel his face flush and he let out a growl, exerting his will into his shoulders. Slowly the sofa began to slide behind him toward the door. The wooden legs squealed as they scraped across the wooden floor. When his growl had used all of the air his lungs held, the movement stopped. Sweat was beading on his face and his legs and shoulders were on fire. Before his momentum was lost, Cameron pulled in a chest full of air through his clenched teeth and let out another explosive growl as he extended his legs from his body in a fluid thrust. Then he had met his limit. He could push himself no farther from the wall.

Cameron rolled over onto his hands and knees and looked down the length of the sofa, still too far from the door. The sofa would need to be no more than a hands length from the metal door to form a proper barricade. Time was running out to restrict the door from opening enough to stop someone from entering. There was more yelling and then automatic weapons fire. The yelling stopped instantly and was followed by a crash that came more behind the door downstairs. The gunmen were at the bottom of the stairwell. They would not take that much longer to get up the stairs. The sofa only needed to be moved a little farther to make a difference.

Cameron scanned the room to see if he had missed something. The only other piece of furniture in the room was the table. His blood coursed through him in the terrible rhythm of his heartbeat, intoxicating him with adrenalin. Cameron pushed himself to be focused, mindful of his surroundings, and fully aware of every opportunity and alternative. Of course, the table was the right size. He raised himself up onto his knees, wrapped his hands around the single long leg, and then pulled the table down toward him. The red sash lamp and the Buddha statue fell to the floor. Cameron pushed the tri-stand against the wall and squeezed himself between the tabletop and the sofa. Again, he clenched his teeth and let roll a growl. The position was to his advantage. This time the sofa moved quickly behind him. The tabletop crackled against his feet as the sofa slid against the door in one swift motion.

Satisfied, Cameron again rolled over to his knees, swiped his hands together, and then picked up his P226 and stood. No sooner was he on his feet than the handle of the door began to jiggle. In his own commotion, Cameron had not heard them come up the stairs. Without pulling the drapes back, he looked down on the street. In front of the restaurant were two black Cadillac Escalades and outside of each stood an armed man wearing a sport coat and dark sunglasses. On busy Yonge Street, the Escalades and these professional gunmen did not turn any heads.

CHAPTER 27
TORONTO

Cameron made his way through the kitchen toward the back of the apartment. Through the wall, he heard the quick creaking steps as other gunmen joined their comrades outside the door.

In the bedroom, Cameron found the others huddled by the French door to the deck. Ananda pressed the thin drape against the glass and craned his neck to view what he could of the courtyard behind the restaurant.

"What do you see down there?" asked Cameron.

Nicole answered for the old man. "We saw one of the gunmen out in the yard. He went back under the deck."

"I do not see him now. Perhaps he is gone," said Ananda.

"He's not gone, he's guarding the door. We'll have to go through him," said Cameron. A deafening thud came from the front of the apartment. The dull, heavy sound was startling and unnatural. "Don't worry, it's going to take them some time to break that door down." Another thud came, followed by another, then another.

Cameron stepped up next to Ananda and craned his own neck to seek out the guard. "I'll have to go out there to get a better look," said Cameron. He slipped his hand behind the drape, unlatched, and then opened the French door wide enough to fit his upper body. Leading with his P226 held high, Cameron leaned out the door. He looked down on the deck to choose where to place his first step. Between the boards of the deck, Cameron could see the courtyard below. The gunman was standing below the edge of the deck.

Cameron froze and then turned his head toward the roof of the building. The building to his right was at least four stories and though the next three buildings to the left were only two floors high, the last building on the corner looked to be about fifteen. Cameron pulled himself back into the apartment and pushed the door shut. "OK, I spotted him. Escaping by rooftop is unlikely. The buildings around us are too tall. I'm pretty sure I can take him out but we will have to move quickly. There are steps around the end of the deck. You can get down that way. I will take a more direct route."

The thudding stopped.

"Why have they stopped?" asked Nicole.

"That was quicker than I thought," said Cameron.

Marie looked to the front of the apartment, "You think they have given up already?"

"Oh, they haven't given up. They just moved to plan B a lot sooner than I thought they would. We have to move now."

Cameron opened the door, looked down through the boards and then out to the rail. He sized up the distance and launched himself out the door. His first step landed mid-deck and propelled him forward to the rail, which he grabbed with both hands, still holding the P226. Using his momentum, Cameron hurled himself over the rail and down onto the gunman below. The gunman heard Cameron's footfall above him and looked up toward the center of the deck. When the gunman realized that Cameron was falling toward him he was too slow to react. He tried to bring his rifle up to block Cameron, sabotaging himself in the process. Cameron's feet pushed the rifle into the gunman's skull, knocking him unconscious before he hit the ground. The blow pushed Cameron back farther than he had intended so he improvised a somersault and finished on one knee, his P226 pointed at the back door of the kitchen.

He could see the kitchen through the closed screen door. There was no movement or sound coming from the bright white room.

Cameron looked at the stairs to his right. Nicole and Marie were waiting at the top holding Lady Mani between them. Lady Yada and Ananda leaned over the railing right behind the other three. Cameron put a finger across his lips and waved them down. He raised himself off his knee, his eyes peering through the door into the kitchen. When the others had joined Cameron he asked Ananda in a whisper, "Is there another way out of this courtyard?"

Ananda shook his head and pointed at the screen door, "Through there."

"OK then, everyone stay close."

Cameron kept his gun leveled at the doorway as he closed in on the screen. He kneeled next to the gunman, unconscious and bleeding on the cement pad, and pulled the rifle from under the gunman's arm. "Put this in that trash can," said Cameron. He handed the rifle to Ananda. Ananda held the rifle at arms length, walked to the trashcan, and deposited the assault weapon as quickly and silently as he could.

Cameron began to step toward the door when he noticed something reflecting the light from near the gunman's waist. Cameron knelt down again and felt toward the object with his fingertips, keeping his eyes on the door. When his fingers found their mark, he wrapped his hand around the object and pulled up a long metal dagger, the same as the one he took off from the assassin in New York. Cameron slipped the dagger into his inside pocket next to the first and then went to the screen door.

Gently Cameron pressed two fingers against the screen and pushed to the side. The screen door opened silently.

He was ready. He would not need to think to shoot.

No one was there to challenge him. The kitchen was empty. Slowly they made their way into the room. The burners were still on, heating skillets and boiling pots. On the grill, vegetables cooked untended. A few more steps and they were almost to the pocket door of the small room leading to the stairwell. Cameron was about ready to peek in when he heard a voice from inside the door. "This will be quick," said the voice. "See, he's finished." Cameron stopped and lifted his hand flat palmed to signal the others to do the same. There were rapid footsteps coming down the wooden stairs, someone running down the steps. Cameron placed the P226 eye level at the edge of the doorframe. If anyone stepped out the doorway of the stairwell, they were finished. Cameron placed his other hand over the one holding the gun to fortify his imminent shot. No one came out of the door. Another voice, different from the first yelled, "Get ready!"

A thunderous blast came from above them. Plaster dust misted from the ceiling. Plan B had been to blow the metal door.

Immediately after the concussion, the sound of quick, creaking steps thumped from inside the doorway. The gunmen were rushing upstairs toward what was left of the metal door.

Cameron was curious as to whether the explosion was enough to push the heavy sofa from behind the door. He did not care enough to stay around to find out. In a fluid motion, Cameron took two quick steps toward the doorway and spun to target anyone unfortunate enough to be standing there. The small room was empty. Everyone that was there a moment before was now getting, or trying to get, into the apartment upstairs.

Cameron pivoted toward the door to the dining room, and as he spun the corner of his eye caught site of something on the floor. Lady Yada gasped. The young man in the shiny blue suit was face-down on the floor, the back of his shiny blue jacket now maroon and dotted with dark red holes. The young man was the person Cameron heard the gunmen interrogating.

Cameron had not doubted these invaders meant business. He was now able to see the business they were in.

CHAPTER 28
TORONTO

Cameron peered quickly out the small porthole window of dining room door to see what they were up against and then quickly pulled his head back. A lone gunman, wearing a sport coat and sunglasses, stood inside the dining room with his back to the kitchen door. The gunman was much taller than Cameron and would be the only resistance until they were outside where at least two more gunmen waited.

"What is out there?" asked Marie, "Are they dead?"

"No. The kitchen staff is seated at the tables with the customers. Everyone looks a little shaken up."

Above them, the thudding started again, this time in short bursts. Cameron was pleased the sofa was causing them delay.

"So we can walk out?"

"Hardly. Wait here a second. I don't want to make a scene out of this."

Cameron pushed open the door, getting the attention of the tall gunman standing guard, though not before Cameron had his P226 pressed into the middle of the gunman's back. Cameron placed his other hand up on the gunman's shoulder, "Ease back, big fella. No need to upset anybody more than we have to."

The gunman said nothing and let Cameron pull him backwards through the kitchen door. The others had lost looks on their faces. The giant in the sport coat dwarfed Cameron, not a small man himself.

"OK, big fella, raise your hands," said Cameron. He reached around to the front of the gunman, grabbed the rifle out of his hands, and tossed the weapon over the counter. Cameron then reached around again and took a heavy .357 from inside the gunman's jacket. He tucked the handgun into his own waist.

The gunman started to slowly turn toward Cameron, his hands still raised. "Hold on," said Cameron.

With his hand to the side of the gunman's chest, Cameron eased the big man around. He frisked the sides of the man's jacket. He felt something on the man's side, pushed him back, and reached again into the man's jacket. From a sheath on the gunman's chest, Cameron pulled another dagger. "Nice," said Cameron, "I'm collecting these."

"Fine, take it," said the gunman. He did not lower his hands. He gave the group a sickly smile. "There is no way you will make it out of here. I will have it back soon enough."

With a lightening blow, Cameron brought the grip of the P226 across the side of the gunman's head. Marie gasped. The eyes of the others went wide.

"Don't be so sure," said Cameron. The giant gunman dropped to his knees. Cameron grabbed the gunman's jacket by the back of his collar, "Get back on your feet. You're going to lead us out of here."

The gunman lumbered back to his feet. "Sure, I'll lead you. But I'll be leading you to your grave."

"Move," said Cameron as he pushed the gunman around to face the dining room door.

"Mr. Kincaid?" asked Marie, "What is the plan?"

"The plan is to waltz out of here and keep going."

When they entered the dining room, all eyes were upon them. Those near them stared in silence while others in the benches whispered amongst themselves. Cameron pushed the gunman forward, shielding his gun inside his jacket. He turned his head slightly back to the others following him. In a low voice Cameron said, "Let's keep moving as fast as we can."

The faces at the tables blurred, the eyes all the same, deep and wide. Cameron scanned the street outside the front of the restaurant. Through the glass wall, he could easily see the same two gunmen standing by the driver's doors of the two black SUVs. The gunmen were looking up and down Yonge Street and not directly at The Lotus Flower.

"We'll need to make this quick," said Cameron. "We only get to do this once."

"Prepare to die," said Cameron's hostage.

Cameron saw a reflection on the glass wall of two men getting up from a table behind him.

Cameron did not hesitate to spin and crack off two shots from his P226. The two men, guns drawn, peered at Cameron with surprise, dark red holes dotting their foreheads. Cameron knew that at least one gunman would be seeded amongst the tourists in the dining room. There had been two.

Cameron's hostage was slack-jawed. Cameron pushed the giant into the glass door, drew the P226 high, and reached for the .357 tucked into his belt. Caught off guard, the gunmen raised their assault weapons. Cameron pointed the handguns to either side of his hostage's head, "Drop them, or your guy gets it first."

Unfazed by Cameron's request the gunmen directed their automatic rifles in his direction.

The giant hostage raised his hands and screamed at his colleagues, "Don't shoot you idiots!" That was the last thing he said before both gunmen opened up on him. With anticipation and without hesitation, Cameron dropped the barrels from the head of the hostage to the gunmen now firing in his direction. He squeezed both triggers, targeting the bridge of the gunmen's sunglasses. The two gunmen fell to their knees at the same time as the hostage they shot. All three were dead. Before the gunmen were flat on the ground Cameron had his hand on the driver's door of the front Escalade.

The others were still clustered inside the door of the restaurant. Cameron waved his free arm back at them, "Let's go!" Lady Yada and Ananda held open the heavy door while Nicole and Marie carried Lady Mani out of the restaurant. All five scurried toward the Escalade. Cameron pulled the driver's door open and pointed the P226 inside. The Escalade was empty and the keys were in the ignition.

The others crossed the sidewalk to the Escalade, huddled in a group.

"Everyone climb in the back," said Cameron. He stuck the .357 back into his belt and reached to pull the back door open.

Nicole was first to climb in. Cameron kept the P226 pointed toward the restaurant. He briefly looked away from the Lotus Flower to see Marie and Lady Yada outside of the Escalade helping Lady Mani up into the seat. Then Cameron noticed for the first time that there was someone in the front passenger seat of the second Escalade parked behind them. The tinted side windows had prevented Cameron from seeing inside the SUV before. The windshield, however, was clear.

"That son of a bitch," said Cameron.

Marie quickly turned her head to Cameron, "What?"

When Cameron did not answer, Marie searched the direction of his gaze. In the front seat of the second Escalade sat Christophe, the waiter from the CN tower. Christophe had given them the symbol they needed to find the Perfect and then he had betrayed them.

Christophe's eyes were on Cameron and Marie. He

had watched them flee the Lotus Flower and now was shocked to see them looking back at him.

"Watch out," said Cameron. He swung the P226 from the direction of the restaurant over Marie's head toward Christophe. Christophe's eyes widened and Cameron's lip curled. Before Cameron could squeeze the trigger three shots rapidly cracked out, coupled with two tinny thuds and a wet thwack near his head. He shifted to see into the Escalade. Nicole was covered in blood, Lady Mani face forward on her lap. Cameron swung his gun back toward the restaurant. No one was there. Another automated burst of gunfire shot down on them and this time Cameron was able to determine that the shots were coming from the second floor. He spun his body around, pulling the .357 out and up with the P226 so that both hands could lock loaded onto the window where the gunman who had fired the rounds was leaning out over the sill. Cameron shot twice, hitting the gunman at least once. Marie slammed the back door and screamed to him, "Mr. Kincaid, drive, drive!" Still looking up, gun pointed high, he pulled himself into the driver's seat. Another gunman pulled the first out of the window and started to lean out. Cameron got two more shots in the direction of the window before turning the key and slamming the truck into gear. He swung his door shut as the Escalade sped away from the restaurant and looked back through the side mirror. Crumpled on the curb were the frail bodies of Lady Mani, Lady Yada, and Ananda, freed from their last lives in this realm.

CHAPTER 29
TORONTO

After the initial shots rained down from above The Lotus Flower, no more followed the black Escalade up Yonge Street, no more gunmen ran out from the crowded restaurant, and the second Escalade, with Christophe in the passenger seat looking on in disbelief, did not pursue Cameron and the women.

Inside the traveling Escalade fast prayers flowed from the back seat in whispers, some words decipherable and others not. The other cars moved slowly or not at all as Cameron maneuvered the Escalade past them. He could hear his heartbeat thumping in his ear and his breaths filled his lungs deeply with sweet air tainted with the fruity scent of the air freshener. A few blocks up, after repeatedly cycling through the side and rearview mirrors, Cameron turned left toward Trinity College. When they reached the parking lot Cameron pulled into the space next to where he had parked the old Chevy.

Cameron exited the Escalade, P226 in hand. He turned quickly in a circle scanning the parking lot around them and the peripheral buildings. Cameron then pulled the handle of the back door. A jolt shot up his arm when the door did not budge, taking his focus from the parking lot to the Escalade. The tinted window blocked his view of the backseat. As he pulled again on the handle, he heard the locking mechanisms switching on and off. Marie was manually unlocking the door, which had automatically locked when they sped from the restaurant.

Cameron turned back toward the parking lot and scanned again while Marie and Nicole climbed out of the Escalade behind him. Satisfied that for the time being they were safe, Cameron reached into the front of the Escalade and took the .357 from the passenger seat where the gun had been tossed. He then tucked both the .357 and the P226 into his waistband, the P226 in the small of his back and the .357 in the front under his flat stomach.

"Into the car," said Cameron. "We have to be quick."

"Agreed," said Marie.

"Why did we stop?" asked Nicole. "Why do we not keep this car?"

"Satellite navigation. One phone call and they can have our location instantly, or shut us down for that matter."

"What is shut us down?"

"The Escalade can be turned off remotely by the satellite system. It's an anti-theft thing."

"Wondrous," said Nicole.

The three opened the doors to the Chevy and climbed in. "Do they not know this car as well?" asked Nicole as she shut the door to the back seat.

"I'm sure they do. We have a better chance with old tech though." Cameron tapped the dashboard. Cameron had thought that through already and was impressed that Nicole had made the connection. Christophe must have identified the Chevy back at the tower and followed them to the restaurant. He was confident the Rex Mundi were so sure their ambush would be sufficient in accomplishing their mission that they arrogantly did not bother leaving anyone behind to guard the Chevy, or Christophe may have followed them alone to the restaurant before alerting his comrades. Either way, the Chevy was free and clear, providing they leave now.

"We can hit 401 north of here," said Cameron. "Do we have a destination in mind?"

"Quebec," said Nicole.

"Quebec, really?"

Marie answered for Nicole, "There are others there that will help us and can transport Nicole to the safety of the Nova Scotia countryside where she will be guarded by the brotherhood."

"The brotherhood, what do you mean? A fellowship of Cathari?"

"Not exactly. These men are chevaliers like you, Mr. Kincaid. Knights whose order has been to take care of the treasure in times of strife for 800 years."

Cameron began cycling through the mirrors again, tapping on the steering wheel with the ends of his fingers while he did. "Knights, brotherhoods, others that can help. I have to say that my experience over the last few days has me less than drawn in."

Nicole continued her prayers in the backseat.

Marie's voice was calm. "I am sorry, Mr. Kincaid. Truly. We could not foresee all that would happen on this journey. There was no way for us to know that the paths of the *Parfaits* would end that way. You have to believe though…"

"I don't have to believe anything," Cameron interrupted. "The others that were to help you have all ended up dead or gone, including those sweet old people we left on the sidewalk in front of the restaurant."

Marie stayed silent only for a moment and then continued with no difference in her tone, "You have to understand, then." On hearing this, Cameron's lips drew tight and he felt his teeth sliding across each other. Seeing him relent, or at least appear to be listening, Marie repeated herself, "You have to understand, that though the details of our journey still remain a mystery to Nicole and myself, the path is foretold as it has been for others since the time of Christ. What you see as tragedy the Holy Spirit has determined. The *Parfaits* were pure and left the husks that housed them to return to the realm of our Lord. Nicole will get to the end of this journey and when her time comes, she will leave this realm for the next as well."

"Even now, after all of this, you still think so?" Cameron wiped the moisture from under his nose and then pulled his hand away, expecting to see blood. There was none.

"Even more now, Mr. Kincaid. We did not truly know that you were chosen as our protector, until now."

"In for a penny, in for a pound," Cameron said in a lighter voice.

"Excuse me, Mr. Kincaid?"

"Oh, something my grandmother used to say. Listen, I gave you my word I would see you safe, and though this is more than I bargained for, I will see it through. Quebec it is. We'll stop at the cabin again on the way through and get some rest. Does that sound OK with you?"

"Yes, Mr. Kincaid, that sounds quite OK."

CHAPTER 30
LAKE ONTARIO

The prayers continued as the Chevy drove back up the lakeside. Cameron listened to the rise and fall of Nicole's whispers, oddly harmonious with the drone of the roadway. Hours had passed before he realized that he was not sure how far they had come. The adrenalin from earlier combined with the trancelike serenity of the long drive had held him in a state of vacuity. With the adrenalin finally spent, he was suddenly aware of the force of cool air blasting across his chin from the A/C vents and that his cheek was almost numb with cold. He reached over to the culprit vent between the dashboard and the window and flipped the fins so that the air was no longer blowing in the direction of his face. Then he pulled his hand up to the bridge of his nose to lightly and quickly massage his eyes beneath their lids. He may as well have been sleeping since they left Toronto and, thinking that was not too safe, decided that they should pull over soon so that they could stretch their legs.

Cameron took the next exit and drove the Chevy into the parking lot of a grocery store. Marie was sleeping and Cameron thought she needed the rest. In the rearview mirror he could see Nicole sitting with her back upright and her eyes closed chanting a prayer in the same rise and fall of whispers that she had since they drove out of Toronto. There was no point in Cameron asking her to join him in the market, as he was pretty sure she was not even aware the Chevy had stopped. He reasoned that if she wanted to stretch her legs she would and proceeded to open his door and get out of the car.

When Cameron stood, he instinctively wanted to stretch. As soon as his brain sent signals through his body to do so, his body responded with a thousand messages from his extremities to let him know that a long time had passed since he'd been a practicing commando. Stopping to stretch had been a good idea. Getting a run in later may be an even better one.

In the market Cameron found what he was looking for, a fresh Lake Ontario brown trout, the size of his thigh, with brilliant yellow-lined black speckles on a field of orange. Marie and Nicole said they ate fish. This Brownie would do fine for dinner. For vegetarian cuisine, Cameron picked out some asparagus and ginger root and the makings for pesto-stuffed mushrooms. Along with a raid of Pepe's wine, he had the makings of a fine dinner that could put this insane day behind them.

When Cameron walked out of the market, the dusk of the sky had shifted to night. Marie was still sleeping, Nicole was still praying, and the cabin was close.

CHAPTER 31
LAKE ONTARIO

The Chevy's headlights lit the back wall of the cabin, as they had when they passed through on their way to Toronto. When the ignition switched off the sudden silence consumed Cameron. Nicole had stopped praying and had been staring out at the darkness for some time. In the silence, the cabin was stuck out of time. All that had happened since they left the lakeshore this morning did not affect the cabin timbers in front of them or the trees by their sides. Even the one sound that came when Cameron opened the Chevy door, the crashing of the waves against the stone break wall that shot out from the shore, was the same as when he had closed the door mere hours before. The waves were the same rhythm, the same tempo. The waves roll in, the waves roll out.

Cameron swung his leg out of the door and onto the ground. Nicole was getting out of the backseat. He turned his head back to Marie. Marie's face and blouse were a shade of amber under the tarnished dome light. She was still sleeping. Why not? This had been a long day if ever there was one. Cameron reached up and rubbed her shoulder, "Hey there, wakey-wakey, we're back at the cabin." Marie did not stir. Cameron turned his head to Nicole in the backseat, still slowly getting out of her door.

"Nicole, why don't you give it a try?" asked Cameron.

"Marie," said Nicole in a singsong voice, "We are back at the cabin."

Cameron walked around to the back of the car to get the groceries from the trunk. "Mr. Kincaid, you had better come here," said Nicole, her voice now serious. When Cameron closed the trunk, he saw that Marie's door was open and that Nicole was standing next to her.

"What is it?" asked Cameron as he walked around the side of the car.

Nicole stepped back and pointed at the seat. Cameron could see a dark spot across Marie's leg that continued down the side of the seat to the floorboard. "Take this," said Cameron, handing the grocery bag to Nicole. With one arm around the front of Marie's shoulder and his other hand on her back, Cameron gently eased her forward so that he could see her back in the light. Nicole gasped. Above Marie's right kidney was a dark red hole, a bullet hole surrounded by blood, dried from bleeding out over the last few hours. Cameron slid his arm behind her, tilted her back, and threw his other arm under her legs.

Cameron lifted Marie out of the Chevy and turned toward the cabin.

Nicole began to speak. "Has she…"

"No," said Cameron abruptly, "she has not gone on to the next life."

Cameron carried Marie into the cabin and took her directly over to the dining table.

"What do we do, Mr. Kincaid?" asked Nicole.

"In the drawer, next to the sink, you'll find some rags. Grab them and then fill that pot on the stove with warm water." Cameron ripped open Marie's blouse and pulled the fabric away from her. In the cabin light, he could now see that she had become pale with the loss of blood. Cameron could also see the exit wound was small and almost directly across from the entry wound. A small exit wound was a good sign that may mean that the bullet had not fragmented and might have just passed through. Still Marie had obviously lost a lot of blood and not mentioning the wound had put her at great risk.

Nicole brought handfuls of rags over to the table. Cameron quickly grabbed them en masse to wipe away the dried blood from Marie's side.

"Why did she not say anything?" asked Nicole.

"From the looks of this wound, she may not have realized it. The wound is clean through and our adrenaline was pretty high. Knowing your mistress, though, she probably kept it to herself so as not to risk me stopping before we were safely away. I wouldn't put it past her." Cameron looked up at Nicole, his hands still busy. "I have never met anyone like Marie. I have known hardened men that were nowhere near as stoic." Cameron looked back down at Marie. "The water, I need the water."

CHAPTER 32
LAKE ONTARIO

After cleaning and dressing Marie's wound, Cameron moved her to the sofa. He watched her breathe perchance she would awake. She did not. Cameron sipped his coffee. When he bought the beans at the grocery store he had thought the coffee would be a nice treat after a good night's sleep. He had poured several cups over the course of the evening. There had been no reason for him to have imagined that as Marie slept in the Chevy her life was slipping away. How could he? She had remained silent. She had not said a word.

Cameron could not decide if Marie's skin color looked better, more flushed. She was still breathing though, and that was something.

Hues of fuchsia edged over the horizon. Cameron propped a throw pillow next to Marie's face to block the morning light soon to come.

At the end of the sofa, Nicole kneeled in meditation. Nicole had spent the better part of the evening praying softly and had gone into a near-trance an hour ago. In the wee hours of the morning, Cameron had suggested that she eat something. Nicole told Cameron that she had begun to fast, so he did not prepare any food for either of them. Now Cameron wished he had. Not because he was hungry, rather because cooking was one of the few things that distracted him.

With the sun coming up Cameron headed out into the yard. With him, he brought the cordless phone from the cabin.

Cameron dialed Pepe's number and Pepe answered on the first ring.

"Cameron," said Pepe. "What are you doing up so early?"

Pepe's quick response threw Cameron for a second, and then he realized that of course Pepe would recognize the number to his own cabin.

"It's a bit much to explain," said Cameron. "I'm sorry if I woke you, I guess I'm preoccupied."

"Wake me? I am just getting in."

"Same ole Pepe."

"Heh, heh. So, what is on your mind that has you so preoccupied? Was your rendezvous not a success? I did not hear of any jazz bars exploding in Toronto last night."

"The rendezvous was not a success, at least not the second part," said Cameron.

"Are the women still with you?"

"Yes, we barely made it out of Toronto with our lives. Marie still might not make it."

"What condition is she in?" asked Pepe, his tone flat.

"A gut shot. It looks clean through and apart from the loss of blood her color is normal."

"Then she is lucky. It may not be septic. Did you find everything you need to dress the wound?"

"Yeah, I found what I needed. It's a waiting game now. That's not why I'm calling though."

"Of course not," Pepe's voice elevated again, "you want to finish this, eh?"

"That's right. I'm tired of playing defense and want the next strike. I have a feeling I can get to them in

Quebec. Are you in?"

"I am, Vive La Légion, count me in," said Pepe.

"Do you want to know the details?"

"Has that mattered before? You can tell me when you see me."

"I knew I could count on you, my brother," said Cameron, and he meant what he said not only because of the shared camaraderie of the French Foreign Legion. He meant those words because he knew Pepe was a stand-up man who really would not need the details until necessary. Pepe was certainly right that the details had never mattered before, not when a brother reached out for assistance.

Cameron added, "We may need a few things —"

Pepe cut him off, "You will find everything we need behind the shed. The key is in the kitchen."

"Perfect."

"Call me when you're ready, I'll be waiting. Vive La Légion, old friend."

"The Legion is our Strength," said Cameron and then switched off the phone.

Cameron was glad he called Pepe. Marie's fate was out of his hands. To take her to a hospital would only have put her in further danger, he was sure of that, and he had already done everything a trauma team would do. Cameron's elite training for treating bullet wounds was certainly better than any the staff would have received in a country hospital. As he had told Pepe, all he could do now was wait. That did not mean Cameron had to wait silently. Behind the shed, Cameron was confident he would find an arsenal sufficient for what he planned next: Going after Rex Mundi.

CHAPTER 33
LAKE ONTARIO

At the edge of the trees, behind the cabin, stood a double-door tool shed. The shed's red paint was dulled and worn from the lakeside winters. Cameron thought that the shed might be older than the cabin, as there would not have been any reason to build a new shed when the larger structure was replaced. That was as much interest as Cameron cared to take in the shed. He was far more interested in what lay on the other side.

Short pines hugged the sides of the shed too close and tight to walk through. Not far to the side, a clear path led into the woods. The path took him around and behind the red shed, where he found an opening in the trees, hidden from the tree line. The floor of the still glade was covered with loose dried pine boughs, some withered brown and others still green. In the center of the glade, barely perceptible from beneath the boughs, was a large circular metal door.

Cameron inspected the clearing's edge. Around the circumference of the open area, a thin wire hovered barely above the ground. Cameron stepped over the wire so as not to trip whatever trap Pepe had set. Either tripping the wire would engage some type of secondary lock or set off an explosion. Knowing how Pepe liked to blow things up, the wire would probably trigger both.

Cameron cleared the nested dried boughs from the circular door with the same care with which he entered the clearing. He found no additional triggers. The key that Cameron brought from the kitchen fit the padlock on the door, as Pepe had described. The door pulled up with ease, the hinges counterbalanced to relieve the weight of the heavy steel. Below, triggered by the open door, a light flickered on, illuminating a narrow metal stairwell.

Cameron cautiously descended the stairs into the cement-walled bunker.

There was no odor in the dimly lit cavity beneath the stairs, no smell of the damp underground, or mold or decay. Still, the air was off.

The lamp the door had triggered was on a metal box mounted on the wall at the bottom of the stairwell. On the side of the box was a lever. Cameron pulled the lever, turning off the lamp and turning on ceiling lights in the room where he stood and in the two rooms adjoining the first. Floor-to-ceiling shelves stacked with dried foods, water bottles, batteries, and rice filled the room. Through the door to the far room, Cameron could see green-blanketed bunk beds, part of a bookshelf, and an elaborate radio built into a desk. The near room held what Cameron was seeking, Pepe's arsenal. Everything a commando could want and more. Against the wall was a gun cabinet. Pressed in foam under glass were the blue metal mini assault weapons he knew as well as his own hands. Cameron chuckled at the thought of Pepe securing the nearly impossible-to-get array of weapons. He slid open the glass to take one of the guns from the foam they were seated in. The little SG carbine felt light and natural. The silenced MP5's, the model Cameron was requisitioned as a commando, and SIG 552's were contraband. Across the side of the 552 in large white letters were the words

"RESTRICTED FOR LAW ENFORCEMENT/GOVERNMENT USE AND/OR EXPORT ONLY." Wherever Pepe found these weapons, they looked authentic. Stored next to the assault rifles were a GL 5140 grenade launcher and two trillium-illuminated night sights, both illegal to possess outside of a government organization. In the drawers, below the glass case, Cameron found cartridges, grenades and, in the bottom drawer, C4 packed in neat little cakes. He even found a case of leather-sheathed Opinel penknives, the type issued by the Legion.

Cameron sorted through Pepe's armory to put together enough weapons and explosives to take on a small army. He gathered what he had separated out into duffel bags, brought the bags out to the Chevy, and stowed them in the trunk.

CHAPTER 34
LAKE ONTARIO

When Cameron finished packing the trunk of the Chevy with the fruits of Pepe's arsenal he sealed up the bunker and went back into the cabin by way of the lakeside deck. The glare from the sun, now above the lake, made the inside of the window-walled cabin hard to see.

When Cameron opened the cabin door, he perked up. Marie was reclining on pillows and talking to Nicole. He stepped inside the door then paused. He started to speak and stopped himself, aware all too quickly that Marie and Nicole were not having a discussion. Nicole was performing the consolamentum. Marie had explained to Cameron that there were only two ways believers could receive the consolamentum. To be deemed worthy after a long period of preparation and instruction as Nicole had or as a request on the deathbed. Cameron knew that Marie had requested the consolamentum because she believed she was dying.

Words and actions passed in and out of Cameron's mind without escaping his silent pose.

When Cameron heard the words, "I have this will, pray to God for me that he will give me his power," come from

Marie's lips, he recited his part from memory to ensure the sacrament was complete. "Good Christian," said Cameron, "I pray you, by the love of God, that you grant this blessing, which God had given you, to our friend here present."

Then as Nicole had the day before, Marie took her vow, "*Parcite Nobis.* For all the sins, I have ever done in thought, word, and deed. I ask pardon of God, of the Church, and of you all."

Nicole and Cameron responded, "By God and by us and by the Church, may your sins be forgiven and we pray God to forgive you them. *Adoremus, Patrem et Filium et Spiritum Sanctam.*"

The humble beliefs that these two women shared were not Cameron's own. Still, he was compelled to speak at the completion of the ceremony perchance they were right. He listened more closely today than yesterday to the passages of the book of John as Nicole recited them. Cameron wanted to believe, for their sakes, Marie and Nicole's, that they were right.

* * * * *

When Nicole finished the Lord's Prayer, she shared an embrace with Marie, and then moved back to the end of the sofa to pray.

Cameron approached Marie and knelt by her side.

Marie's forehead beaded with sweat, her mouth held the courage of a warm smile.

"Can I get you anything to eat?" asked Cameron.

"No, thank you, Mr. Kincaid," said Marie, her voice soft and weak.

"It's Cameron, Marie, Mr. Kincaid is not necessary. Let me get you something, please. Some food will build up your strength."

"Cameron," said Marie. He smiled when she called him by his first name. "You know I will not be getting any stronger. I have begun the endura. I will no longer eat or drink. The fasting will speed my departure to heaven."

Cameron's brow furrowed and he inhaled deeply through his nose. Marie continued, "It's really quite all right. Nicole has prepared me and I am now one with the Holy Spirit."

Cameron leaned forward to kiss her forehead, "You must not kiss me. I must remain pure."

"Will you become a Perfect now?" asked Cameron.

"I am going to die, but now that I am truly pure, I will be able to go to heaven."

The two looked at each other for a long moment. Finally, Marie said, "You know, Monsieur Claude was right."

"How's that?"

"There is something about you, a *je ne sais quoi* that has led to a charmed life."

They both chuckled lightly. "I don't feel very charmed right now," said Cameron.

"But you are. You are the chevalier that has been chosen to protect the treasure."

"I don't know what you mean."

"Nicole is the treasure you must protect. You must protect her and deliver her to safety."

"You mean because only she has knowledge of the treasure?"

"No, Cameron, I am telling you that Nicole is the treasure you must protect."

"I don't understand, you said there were other Perfects."

"This is true, but Nicole is very special to us."

"How so?"

"Remember, if a Perfect loses austerity, even in the slightest, if they should eat meat or willfully kiss, then they lose the power of the sacrament. More so, all of those that have received the consolamentum along the line of that Perfect also lose the power of the sacrament. Nicole will continue a line that we know to be pure and uncorrupted, all the way back to our Lord Jesus. She is special to us because only with the sacrament can we escape the cycle of rebirth in this physical realm and return to heaven from which we all came. She is our salvation."

"The salvation of the Cathar?"

"Not only the Cathar, for all people, for you. Salvation is not in this world, not in simple belief, not in the walls of a church. The gift of the Holy Spirit Nicole carries is all that is needed to bring peace to all mankind, to end the cycle of suffering of this world. To deliver all of God's children from the trickery of this world to their rightful place in heaven."

"So she is the treasure that the Rex Mundi are after? The treasure they think will change the world?" asked Cameron.

"She carries with her our only sacrament. When the time is right, the Cathar will again spread the true religion. People will learn that the material world is false, that the churches, mosques, synagogues are all merely manifestations of the material world. The great lie. When people learn that the Holy Spirit is easily attained with pure living, and that there is no reason for fear or wealth and that there is a way to be freed from this world, from this cycle, that will change the world."

"That's a lot to take in. I thought the treasure was a cavern of gold and jewels or some secret royal bloodline."

"Salvation is the treasure the Rex Mundi fear. The gold and bloodline are of their world, things they can manipulate and control. The truth will always be the truth, so for them it must be kept secret and ultimately destroyed." Marie looked down at Nicole at the end of the sofa. "Nicole, dear. Come here," said Marie.

Nicole stopped her prayer and came closer to Marie.

Marie reached her hands around to the back of her head. The emerald pendant slid up her neck as she teased the ends of the necklace. Marie's eyes squinted and she let out a sigh.

"Let me help you," said Nicole, and she reached

behind Marie's neck to unfasten the clasp. After Nicole separated the clasp, she put the necklace into Marie's hands and gently closed Marie's hands around the pendant. Nicole rested her own hands on the edge of the sofa. Marie lifted the pendant and reached around Nicole's neck. Marie's hands fumbled again and as the two shared a smile. Nicole reached up to refasten the clasp.

Cameron wanted to ask why the necklace was so important. Marie had impressed upon him the Cathar's view of the physical, the essence of which was that the physical is a lie and has no value or spiritual worth. Yet, the look in Marie's eyes as she gave the pendant to Nicole signified that there was something special about the necklace. Cameron decided not to beat upon the obvious negation. The belief Marie and Nicole had in the physical realm was not Cameron's own, or even his business.

CHAPTER 35
QUEBEC

Cameron powered up his cell phone. To conserve the battery he had left the phone off since leaving Montreal. He was glad to see that the little battery icon in the corner of the screen was still green. On the seat next to him was a piece of paper with a phone number that Marie had given him, the number to the Cathari in Quebec.

Marie had thought that the gunshot wound was fatal and had requested the consolamentum to be become a Perfect before dying. Anticipating imminent death, she had even begun the endura, a form of voluntary euthanasia through starvation. Believing she was mortally wounded, Marie would refuse to eat or drink to speed death. Cameron thought she had gone to an unnecessary extreme receiving the last sacrament. The bullet had gone clean through, and though Marie had lost a great amount of blood, she had regained consciousness and her color had returned. Cameron thought she was on the upswing and was preparing the thigh-sized brown trout he bought from the market on the drive from Toronto when Nicole came from the sofa to tell him that Marie had passed. Cameron had been so sure that Marie was going to recover that he had put on classical music while he was cooking and opened a bottle red wine. Cameron thought that all he needed to do to convince her to take some nourishment was to prepare an irresistible meal. Marie had not lived to see the meal served.

Now driving north on highway 401 back toward Montreal, Cameron had taken over Marie's task. He would contact the Quebec safe house that was waiting for the young Perfect, the Cathari treasure.

Cameron handed Nicole the paper, "Read that number to me." He lifted his cell phone over the steering wheel so that he could enter the number and still see the road. As Nicole read the phone number to Cameron, he punched the digits into the phone. He placed the cell phone next to his ear and waited for someone to pick up. The answer came quickly.

Though they said nothing, Cameron knew that somebody had answered because of the click. He said the two words Marie had given him to make contact, "White swan."

He was curious to see if he would even get a response or if the phone would go dead.

"Hello," came a voice on the other end of the line. Cameron knew the voice on the line, though he was unsure of the meaning of Christophe answering the phone.

"Hello," said Cameron.

"There is nowhere to go. Nowhere safe, at least, and you're a fool if you think so."

"Is that so?"

"Really, you have to ask. I would have thought that by now you would have abandoned those witches."

Christophe had said witches, plural, that told Cameron that the Rex Mundi was unaware that Marie had been wounded, that Marie had died. "I can honestly say that the thought has crossed my mind," said Cameron.

"You know you can still walk away. We only want the young woman."

"And why is that?"

"She is dangerous. Mostly to you right now," said Christophe.

"Thank you for your deep concern for my well being."

"Listen, we could care less what you do after you hand over the young woman. We will not follow you. We will even make it worth your while, and then, you will be done, your hands free."

"How much do you figure the young woman is worth?" asked Cameron.

"Bring us the young woman and we will give you five hundred thousand dollars."

"Woo, that might make it worth my while. I bet you fellas have deeper pockets than that. Let's make it an even million. Whadda you say?" asked Cameron. He expected Christophe to argue. Christophe did not. Rather, he answered without hesitation.

"A million it is," said Christophe.

"And all I have to do is hand over the young woman."

"That's right, all you have to do is hand over the young woman. We don't even care about the other one. We only want the young one."

"Fine," said Cameron. "Where can we make the switch?"

Cameron could hear Christophe talking to someone else, another man, as clear as if that person were on the phone as well. Though Christophe had not hesitated at the price, he was caught off guard at Cameron's acceptance.

"You are in Quebec?" asked Christophe. That was another good sign. The operatives did not know where Cameron was.

"Where do you want to do the exchange? It will need to be someplace public."

"Public, of course," said Christophe. "You know the Notre Dame Cathedral?"

"Yes, I know where that is."

"Good. Be there tomorrow at noon."

"Noon tomorrow, got it."

"And Mr. Kincaid…"

"Yes," said Cameron. He thought Christophe might have heard Marie or Nicole call him by that name at the restaurant — so much for anonymity.

"If you have a change of heart, may I remind you once again, there is nowhere to run."

"Oh, my mind is decided," said Cameron. "Don't worry yourself about that." Cameron pulled the cell phone from his ear and hit the end call button.

"What are you doing?" asked Nicole. "I cannot believe you plan to betray us. I mean, Marie would be so upset." Nicole turned her head to look out her window.

"You are right not to believe that I would betray you. I won't. I will do what I need to do to draw them out though. They're so predictable. We'll use that to our advantage."

"What do you mean predictable?" asked Nicole.

Cameron turned toward her and arched his brow. "Really?" said Cameron. Since Nicole became a Perfect in Toronto, she had been praying constantly and only drinking water for nourishment. Cameron thought that Nicole might be in shock.

"Yes, really. What is predictable that we can use?"

Cameron was looking back to the road. "What I mean by predictable is that these Rex Mundi have been around every corner we have turned." His hand, still squeezing the cell phone, tapped some invisible object above the dashboard. "Predictable is that when I called that number Marie gave me, a number, by the way, that was supposed to be to a safe house in Quebec, it was not one of the good guys that answered the phone." Cameron flashed his eyes away from the road to Nicole. "Christophe answered the phone. Christophe, who only two days ago, mind you, was outside the Lotus Flower in Toronto, is now already in Quebec."

"So?"

"In Quebec, Nicole. He could have been in any city in

North America, or any of the other safe houses. He wasn't, he was in Quebec. The Rex Mundi not only knew about the safe house." Cameron let the next word out slow and heavily enunciated, "Again." He flashed another look to Nicole this time with his brows arched high, "They knew that was our next destination."

"You're right. That is strange."

"Strange, yes that is a word for it, strange. Odd might be another word. A better word might be intel, as in 'good intel on their part.' You said yourself they have had years to track your movements, waiting for an opportunity to strike, never giving up their hand. That makes them predictable. They will be where they expect us to be. So we will not disappoint, we will go right to Quebec as planned. They will be waiting for us and when we get there we will simply deal with them, and then be on our way." Cameron turned his head one last time and winked.

"You can not deal with the operatives of Rex Mundi," said Nicole.

"I suspect we can."

"When they see me, they will kill me."

"When I say we, I do not mean the two of us."

CHAPTER 36
QUEBEC

Drops of rain blotted out the windshield as fast as the wipers cleared the glass. Cameron's eyes had become sore over the last hour. The pounding patter of the rain abruptly stopped as the Chevy drove under the roof of the gas station. Rather than stop first at the gas pumps, Cameron pulled the Chevy into a parking space near the doors of the mini-mart. Cameron rolled the window down, flooding the car with the cool damp of rain and gas fumes. Nicole could not make out the figure that walked over to Cameron's window. He moved too quickly. Still, Nicole knew the man before he spoke.

Pepe leaned into the window, his portly face filling the frame, "*Bonne journée, mes amis, demoiselle, Kincaid.*" He looked over Cameron's shoulder to the backseat, "*Dame Marie?*" Cameron subtly shook his head without turning toward Nicole. Pepe frowned and then let his smile return. He held his hands up to the window. Each held a coffee. "One for each of you," said Pepe. He looked past them to the rain falling hard beyond. "It's a good day for hot coffee." Cameron took the coffees and offered one to Nicole. "*Non, merci,*" said Nicole. Cameron handed the cup back to Pepe.

"She's fasting." Pepe took the cup. "I'm not," he said. He shrugged and then stepped to the back door of the Chevy and got into the dry backseat.

"*Excusez-moi pour un moment,*" said Nicole as she opened her door.

"You OK?" asked Cameron.

"Yes, I need to…" her eyes widened round.

"— Certainly, yeah, go ahead."

Nicole closed the door and went into the mini-mart. Pepe leaned up to the front seat, "So *demoiselle* is OK?"

"Yeah, she's OK. As far as she is concerned, Marie is in a better place."

"Maybe," Pepe sighed. "When you called you sounded optimistic for the other one. I thought you said the wound was clean."

"She lost too much blood." Cameron sipped his coffee, then moved the cup in front of his mouth and lightly blew into the opening. "Plus she would not eat."

"Would not eat?"

"Yeah, the endura she called it. She had Nicole give her, well, sort of a last rite, a bit much to describe really, and then refused to eat or drink anything. The endura is the express to heaven."

"So it worked."

"I guess it did."

"So this one is religious? Perfect."

"In so many words. That's what this whole thing is about. Marie and Nicole are Cathari — were, are —anyway, Nicole is now a Cathar holy woman."

"Cathari? Like those New Agers in Languedoc?" asked Pepe.

"How is it everyone knows about Cathari but me?"

"What's to know? My cousin lives near Beziers. There is a huge festival there every July. Everyone is Cathar for a day, wearing T-shirts that say 'Kill them all' and 'Tuez-les tous.'"

"I am out of the loop. Well, yeah, they are Cathari, but

I am led to believe they are the real deal. Old-school, if you will," said Cameron.

"Here I thought all of the Cathari were wiped out in the Albigensian crusade. Did you know that during the crusades thousands of people were killed in an attack on Beziers alone? Indiscriminately, a tragedy."

Cameron turned toward the backseat, "How do you know all this?"

"What? You don't read history?" Pepe tapped the side of his forehead, "That is your problem Cameron, you need to read more."

"I guess I do."

"So it's about religion," Pepe sipped his coffee and lowered his head to look out the side window. "Are we talking terrorists? You know, after that time in Bali I am not so happy with these religious types."

"Not exactly terrorist. Have you ever heard of the Rex Mundi?"

"Kings of the world? You have me there. Are they Cathari too?"

"They are not. The Rex Mundi are the bad guys, and we are going after them."

"Say no more. Did you find everything we need?"

"Right where you said, it's all in the trunk."

CHAPTER 37
QUEBEC

"So are you two going to tell me your plan?" asked Nicole.

"Sure," said Cameron.

"I for one would love to hear it," said Pepe.

"Well, we'll go into Quebec tonight, stay with Pepe's people, and at noon tomorrow Pepe and I will go to the Notre Dame de Quebec. I will go inside and offer you in exchange for our freedom and a million, whatever it is they have." Cameron pursed his lips, "I should have specified US dollars. No wonder Christophe was so quick to answer, I bet he has Canadian currency."

"Why would you betray Marie?" asked Nicole. "The operatives of Rex Mundi cannot be trusted."

"Don't worry, you will be safely hidden away. Surrender is the best way to lure out the Rex Mundi." Cameron looked into the rearview mirror at Pepe, "And if there is one thing the French have taught me, it's to become a master at the art of surrender."

Pepe grunted at Cameron's comment and then added softly, "You can relax, Cameron knows what he is doing."

Nicole shook her head, "The Rex Mundi are very

dangerous."

"Surrendering is a tactic," said Pepe. He held up his hands on either side like a scale, "You see, it transforms weakness into power."

"What do you mean?" asked Nicole.

"You know of Voltaire?"

"Yes, he was a French philosopher. Marie tutored me about all of the writers of the enlightenment. Voltaire wrote of religious freedom."

"*Oui,* but you see being a critic of the church got Voltaire into trouble and he was exiled from France. So, he fled to London. Not a popular place to be for a Frenchman at the time."

"Or ever," said Cameron.

Pepe grunted again, "Well, very unpopular at that time. So much so, that one day while walking he found himself surrounded by people screaming 'hang the Frenchman, hang the Frenchman!'"

"If I had a dime for every time I heard that," said Cameron.

"True," said Pepe. He gave Cameron a quick leer and then let his face rest pleasant again to continue his story. "So Voltaire, seeing he was surrounded and outnumbered, thought quickly, and instead of trying to fight the Englishmen, he used his wit. He said 'Men of England! You wish to kill me because I am a Frenchman. Am I not punished enough in not being born an Englishman?' at which the crowd laughed and safely escorted him home." Pepe arched his brow. "So you see, Voltaire both took advantage of their weakness and made power of his weakness by surrendering, not fighting."

"The Cathar know this well," said Nicole. "I am glad to hear that you do not intend to fight them."

"I did not say that," said Pepe. "I said Voltaire chose not to fight. We will fight."

CHAPTER 38
QUEBEC

After two days of rain, billowy clouds now floated across the Quebec's azure sky. Cameron had spent the morning walking through the Parc de l'Esplanade thinking about Marie and the last few days. Now he sat on a bench in the small park across Rue Sainte-Felixine from the Notre Dame de Quebec. Cameron gazed up at the facade. Pepe told him that the Quebec basilica was modeled after the one in Paris and that Cameron would recognize the building when he saw it. Pepe was right, the church did look a lot like the Sainte-Geneviève in Paris. Sainte-Geneviève was a church near the hotel Pepe and Cameron used to stay in years before while on a leave from the Legion. Those early days, Cameron and Pepe caroused through Paris with Pepe's sister Christine and her friends. Of course there had been Christine. The European architecture of that part of Quebec reminded Cameron of his time spent abroad.

High above the church steeple the sun hit the zenith of the celestial arc. High noon and time to turn over Nicole. The Rex Mundi were expecting him. Cameron stood up from the bench and ran his fingers down the length, pulling the collar tight when his hands neared the bottom.

Cameron flexed his neck, rolling his head back and to the side.

From his inside pocket Cameron removed his cell phone and tapped the power on. Scanning the street, he tried to identify anyone waiting for a call. No one looked particularly out of place. Two women deep in conversation were pushing strollers side by side. A young man, maybe a student Cameron thought, chained his bicycle to the signpost near the wrought-iron gate. At the bottom of the basilica steps, a group of middle-aged tourists in baggy shorts stood with cameras and guidebooks in hand. When the phone powered up Cameron scrolled through his outgoing messages to the number he called yesterday on the drive up to Quebec. He held the phone to his ear and waited for someone to pick up. Cameron was not disappointed.

"*Bonjour,*" said a voice on the phone, not Christophe this time. Cameron recognized the voice just the same. The voice was that of the man Christophe was talking with yesterday when he thought that Cameron could not hear him.

"It's midday," said Cameron.

"So it is," said the man in a matter-of-fact tone. "The last confessional booth."

The line was dead.

Cameron sighed. He slipped the cell phone back into his inside pocket, dropped his arms to his sides, and then stretched his fingers wide. No one around him had picked up a phone, taken any notice of him, or made any casual steps toward the door of the basilica. Cameron spoke under his breath, his lips barely trembling, "Here goes nothing. I'm going in."

"Have fun at mass," said Pepe. Cameron heard him in the tiny earpiece resting just inside his ear canal.

Cameron stepped to the curb and lightly touched down onto the small lane separating the church from the park, "It will only be confession today, my friend."

"That could fill the day," said Pepe.

"No, not at all," said Cameron.

"When is the last time you confessed?"

"Never."

"That is a lot of hail Marys, I believe."

"One evil at a time. That's the best I can do."

"Maybe the money is in the confessional," said Pepe.

"Maybe it's a trap," said Cameron.

"That would be dishonest. Which confessional will you be in?"

"He said the last one," Cameron briskly climbed the half a dozen steps up to the promenade.

"The end of the line. I'll be watching. Vive La Légion," said Pepe.

"The Legion is our strength. I'll see you soon."

Cameron walked into the open door beyond the steps, entering a large anteroom that buffered the outside door from the cathedral. The church was tranquil and cool, a departure from the heat and humidity across the promenade. Cameron walked toward the amber light beaming through the door of the anteroom from the cathedral. He took a breath and stepped into the doorway prepared to lock in the details of the room without looking too obvious. Cameron had expected the cathedral to be impressive and was rewarded. A wash of light came down from the portico windows bordering the ceiling to reflect on the golden baldaquin, and the throne dais behind the altar was adorned with royal ornamentation. A few people, more likely pilgrims than parishioners, sat in the first few pews near the door. Others sat sporadically throughout the church.

Cameron strolled up the aisle along the rows of long wooden pews. The deeper Cameron walked into the cathedral the further he was immersed in the smells of antiquities, incense, and varnish that hung in the air. The cabinet-like confessional booths lined the sidewall. The voice on the phone had said to go to the last confessional. When Cameron reached the pew even with the last prayer closet, he turned from the center aisle, nonchalantly scanned the room and balconies for anything out of sorts, and then went to the confessional. Everything in the cathedral appeared appropriate.

CHAPTER 39
QUEBEC

The door to the confessional was open. Cameron thought to let Pepe know he was going into the confessional and decided not to, fearing that, due to the silence of the cathedral, even the faintest voice would carry. He questioned his sanity for entering the confessional booth to begin with, away from the safety of the open cathedral. Pepe had his back, though, and that was reassuring. Cameron stepped into the small wooden booth and fastened the door behind him with the inside latch. Immediately a slatted panel behind the wooden screen separating Cameron from the priest slid open. Cameron waited for someone to speak and when no one did, he said, "Forgive me, father for —." Cameron was interrupted by the voice from the phone. "There is no need for that, Mr. Kincaid," said the voice.

"Have it your way. To whom am I speaking?"

"That does not matter in the least. What does matter is that you seem to have come alone. Excuse the pun, but I pray you are not intending a ruse." Cameron detected a subtle French accent, not Canadian French, or French proper, rather some other dialect.

"I wanted to be sure I had an exit." Cameron did not let his voice waver. "And right at this moment I'm not overwhelmed with confidence."

"Our surroundings?"

"You have to admit, this is a confined space."

"You are right, sir. Feel free to step out into the open if it makes you feel better."

"It will, I assure you."

"Fine, then," said the voice in an upbeat tone.

Cameron reached for the latch to the confessional door.

"Not that way, Mr. Kincaid," said the man behind the screen.

The panel behind the little screen slid shut. From around the edge of the confessional door came a rapid succession of clicks. Cameron was sure these were bolts locking the door in place. He unfastened the latch and pushed, not moving the door in the slightest.

"C'mon, what is this?" asked Cameron.

"What's going on?" asked Pepe.

Cameron was about to respond when the panel behind the little screen opened again, this time slowly and only halfway. Cameron leaned toward the screen. "If you're trying to get on my good side it's not working," said Cameron.

Cameron heard the sound of an aerosol spray through the wooden screen and felt a mist on his face. Suddenly Cameron's eyes were burning. Pepe spoke again, "Is everything OK? Give me a signal."

Cameron knew better than to try to talk, to even breathe. But for him to resist the gas was futile in the closed space of the confessional. One word and Pepe would have the door in splinters. He tried to speak with no success. The code word was "angel." A word they agreed could be subtly slipped into any conversation Cameron would be having while in the church. Now any sound would suffice, a simple "help" or a rapid tap on the wall. The burning had traveled into his throat and he was unable to make a sound. Cameron decided to alert Pepe by knocking on the wall. His arms were weak and the walls were moving. The walls of the confessional began to melt and ripple. He felt himself falling and placed a hand on the wall in front of him to catch himself and then his other on the sidewall. Bracing himself did nothing to still the spinning box.

Mustering all of his will, Cameron pushed himself back against the wall. His tear ducts flowed heavy and out of his twisted mouth, saliva shot out with each frantic tightening breath. For a moment, Cameron's body seized tight and within his face, he felt his muscles ripping away. He could hear Pepe's voice, nonsense words echoing and reverberating. Cameron separated from his body, only a mind behind eyes floating away from his head, watching the walls spin by as he fell away from them. Then the falling became so extreme Cameron could no longer focus. Everything went black.

CHAPTER 40
QUEBEC

Cameron awoke to total darkness, his muscles burning from the earlier spasms. He tried to lift his hand to his forehead to no avail. When he jerked at his other hand, lightning shot up through his arm into his shoulder. His hands were immovable, bound tight behind his back.

He widened his eyes, still unable to see.

Cameron's instinct kicked in to override his disorientation. He remembered the Rex Mundi, the enemy, subdued him. The epiphany that the Rex Mundi wanted him disoriented snapped him into action. Cameron had been trained for this and he was not about to give them the upper hand. In the Legion, disorientation training began early, before the elite training. Every candidate went through countless rigors after selection in Aubagne. Cameron had gone on to Corsica, home of the elite of the elite, the Second Foreign Parachute Regiment. He had been bound, electrocuted, water boarded — and that was in his first week as a recruit.

Cameron started by measuring his breaths to ensure he was getting enough oxygen. He realized he could only breathe through his nose. As Cameron slowly squeezed his jaw tight he could feel a tug at the base of his skull, the knot of a gag tied tight around his head.

The muscles throughout Cameron's body were still on fire from the aerosol gas. He resisted the temptation to pull or struggle against his restraints. He let his body go limp. Slowly Cameron identified each of his extremities and their positions. Through concentration, he had a good mental picture of his situation. He was sitting on a chair, gagged, hooded, and bound by his hands with no tension on his legs, lap, or waist.

Cameron focused on where he sensed the bindings were tight, around his crossed wrists and behind his back. He determined that the binding on his wrist was what held him to the chair. Fingers loose, Cameron sought to touch whatever he could only to find nothing in their reach. Unable to untie the bindings with his hands or maneuver the Opinel knife from his side, he thought of an alternative. Cameron knew a way out of being single bound from the back, a simple rookie maneuver. All he would need to do is find a way to throw himself back on his own weight, shattering the chair and maybe an arm, to free the bindings and allow him to wriggle loose. Cameron pressed both feet firm. They were solid, and to fall back could work.

The room smelled like a barbecue — maybe this was the furnace room.

Cameron tried to gauge his space. Thwacking his head on the wall behind him might slow his fall and only leave him with a lump. To his right a drip hit a pool, easily a body length away. More important was the faint echo made each and every time a drop landed in the pool. Cameron was definitely not in a room as small as the confessional booth. He closed his mind off from his body and counted between the drops. When Cameron reached five another drip hit the pool. The echo circled him, drip, count five, drip, count five, repeated again and again until Cameron was confident he was in the center of the room. He decided there was plenty of room behind him. There could be debris or a hole waiting for him when he fell back. There could be a bottomless pit, for all he knew. Cameron would take that risk. To not try to free himself was against his training and he had no doubt that the Rex Mundi had no plans of to let him go free.

Applying slight pressure to the front of his feet, Cameron tried to lift the chair to test whether the chair was bolted to the floor and could even be tilted back. The front of the chair lifted. He gently lowered the chair back to the floor. The chair, perhaps built of wood, made a solid thud. Throwing the chair back to free himself was going to work. Cameron pulled his body as far forward as he could manage. Ready to put all of his weight into the thrust back, he tensed his feet.

Above Cameron's head the voice of the man from the phone boomed through speakers, "I wouldn't do that, Mr. Kincaid."

Cameron relaxed his feet and began to sit upright.

"I am glad to see you awake," said the voice.

Cameron decided to take his shot and leaned forward again.

"Really, Mr. Kincaid! I assure you that will not be in your best interest."

The abruptness in the voice jarred Cameron. He sat up again.

"Good, relax for a moment longer. I will join you."

Cameron was not going to relax. He had been ready to throw the chair back to set himself free from his binds. He knew the man's exclamation was sincere — whatever was behind the chair put Cameron's safety in jeopardy. Cameron had no doubt that the man was nowhere near concerned for his future well-being. The man needed him safe until he told the man where to find Nicole.

Cameron heard a door bolt turn behind him, followed by a second. He could even hear the handle turn. He knew when the man entered the room, even though he could not hear the door swing open. Near his head, he heard a pull chain and then suddenly there was enough light for him to see through the fabric of his hood. He could not make out any shapes, only the bright reflection of the light off the wall in front of him.

With a sudden motion, the hood was pulled from Cameron's head. Exposure to the naked light overwhelmed his eyes. Cameron pulled his eyes tightly closed and then opened them widely again, trying to force them into focus. The wall in front of him was warped and moving. Again, Cameron closed and reopened his eyes.

The man spoke, "Sorry about that. It is from the salvia divinorum in the aerosol I used to knock you out. It's an ancient shamanic drug native to the Sierra Mazateca in Oaxaca, Mexico, where it is still used by the Mazatec, primarily to facilitate shamanic visions in the context of curing or divination." Cameron was still unable to focus. The man continued, now standing to the side of Cameron, "thus its name divinorum, which means 'of the ghosts' and should actually be divinatorum, 'of the priests.' Mr. Kincaid, you are not quite snapping out of it. Peter, would you?"

From behind, Cameron heard a snap and then felt soft clammy leather as someone wrapped their hand tightly around his forehead and pulled his head back. Under his nose came a rush of ammonia, burning his eyes and sinuses. Cameron tried to thrash his head to either side, unable to slip from the grip of the gloved hand. The fumes of the ammonia fell away from his face and were replaced by fumes of something milder. The pain subsided and the gloved had released him. To Cameron's right the man snapped his fingers once and then again. Cameron slowly turned toward the sound.

"That's right, Mr. Kincaid, this way."

Cameron's eyes began to focus.

"There you go, Mr. Kincaid, it will be only a minute more. Thank you, Peter. Now where was I, oh yes, salvia divinorum. So, the Mazatec shamans see the plant as an incarnation of the Virgin Mary, and begin the ritual with an invocation to Mary, Saint Peter, the Holy Trinity, and other saints. Of course, in their rituals, they use only the freshest leaves, and you ingested…well, let's just say you ingested quite a different concoction, a requirement, you see. The leaves only last ten minutes and how would I ever get you to eat them?" The man laughed after he made the comment. Cameron did not find the words funny.

CHAPTER 41
QUEBEC

Cameron could now, for the first time, see the man in front of him quite well. Whatever they had shoved in his nose had made him quite lucid.

The man was tall, well groomed, and had a very kind smile. Cameron thought his looks were almost too good, artificial, like a model or an actor. He wore all black with the exception of his white collar. The man was a priest. Cameron's eyes were drawn to the large garnet-set gold ring on the priest's second finger.

"There, you are doing better. I can see it. Peter, can you remove our guest's…" The priest gestured to his mouth. Cameron felt the stiff blade of Peter's knife slide up the side of his head and the pressure when Peter used the blade to cut away the gag. The gag fell away.

"Here, drink this." The priest held a metal cup to Cameron's lips. He tilted the offering into his mouth. The water contained in the cup poured down Cameron's throat and onto his chin and shirt. Cameron sucked down what he could.

When the priest lowered the cup Cameron spoke. "You're a priest."

"Surprised?" said the priest.

"Not really. You did have me meet you in a confessional."

"Well, a lot of priests go through here. It's easy to, what's the word, *comme camouflage*?"

"Blend?" asked Cameron.

"Yes, that's it, it's easy to blend."

The priest pulled a stool from Cameron's side to the front of him and sat. "You see, this is the primate church of Canada, the seat of the Roman Catholic Archdiocese of Quebec, the oldest See in the New World north of Mexico."

"Thank you for the history lesson," said Cameron.

"That's not the best of it all. Four governors of New France and the bishops of Quebec are buried in the crypt, beyond that wall in front of you. That chancel lamp in the cathedral, did you see it?"

"I saw it."

"It was a gift from Louis XIV."

"How special." Cameron was regaining his strength.

"You should have taken the tour. These places, these things, are all very important."

"I recently met someone who would say very different."

"Yes, I know the rhetoric. There are no primates or bishops in the Bible, the physical church and the physical itself should be disregarded." The priest lost his smile and turned his furrowed brow to Cameron adding in a serious tone, "That God himself should be disregarded."

"That's about what I've heard."

"Those are dangerous thoughts, they always have been. You were smart to agree to meet, that woman is a threat that must be dealt with."

"Dealt with? What does that mean, and what happened to the believers that were supposed to be at the number where I called you?"

The priest put his hand on Cameron's shoulder, patted, pulled back and shrugged, "These people you call believers, that call themselves pure ones, good Christians, these *bonnes gens*, these Cathari, whatever name they go by, they are like rats. We exterminate as many as we can but some always get away." The priest shook his head slightly. "We have been watching the local group for a long time, waiting for this opportunity, this precious opportunity, and now it has finally come," the priest clasped his hands together. "Now, Mr. Kincaid, where can we find her?"

Cameron's earpiece came to life. "Kincaid, I am in range. If you can hear me give the signal."

The earpiece was small and flesh-colored, still Cameron was surprised the device had been missed by his captors. "About that," said Cameron, "you will need an angel to help you now."

"Got you, I am on my way," said Pepe.

The priest was less than amused. "I am sorry you feel that it will need to come to that," he said.

Cameron realized now that the reason for the single bind was that his captors had bound him in a rush. They had not even removed his sport coat and with the layers of clothing had missed the P226 tucked in his behind his back and only taken the .357 from his side.

Though the drug in the gas had been incredibly strong, the effects only subdued Cameron briefly, and that made the Rex Mundi sloppy.

"Peter, could you help our friend to understand?"

Cameron was more than excited to know that Pepe was close. Under the circumstance he wanted Pepe to be closer, to be there.

Cameron was not sure what hit him first, the burn of the thin metal wire beside his face or the smell of his own burning flesh.

Cameron clenched his jaw. If he had to, he could do this all day. Where the hell was Pepe?

"So you see, Mr. Kincaid," the priest nodded to Cameron's assailant, "we invented the art of interrogation."

Another stiff wire, glowing red, was thrust into

Cameron's thigh.

Cameron felt the rod deeply and mistakenly let the priest know by gasping.

"You do see." The priest flicked his brow, signaling Peter to step back. The priest lifted himself from his stool and leaned into Cameron, placing a hand on either side of his face.

"The Holy See charged our predecessors, the Dominicans, with establishing the Episcopal inquisition." The priest nodded and Cameron felt the puncture of another skewer, this time he pushed the brilliant flash of pain into a leer toward the priest. The priest continued nonchalantly, holding Cameron's face firmly, studying him. "Before that, heretics were dealt with on a local level, sometimes merely imprisoned. But in the name of the Pope all things changed."

"So you're Dominican. The Rex Mundi is the church?"

"Oh, I didn't say that. Our people are there, though."

Peter lanced Cameron in the thigh once more. The priest, still holding Cameron's face, let loose one hand to caress his burnt cheek.

"Our people have always been everywhere, Mr. Kincaid." The priest moved his caressing hand to Cameron's forehead and then pulled both hands back to his lap. "That's enough for now, Peter," said the priest.

"Ironically this system of, well, let's call it what it is, torture, was created for the predecessors of your friends. For the same reason that we use it today." The priest reached behind Cameron and brought back the metal cup and a matching pitcher. As the Priest spoke, he filled the cup full of water. "The problem is the same. Do you know what that problem is, Mr. Kincaid?"

"I can't say," Cameron winced midsentence and then quickly pulled himself together. "I can't say that I do."

"But of course you don't. Here, drink this." The priest put the cup of water to Cameron's lips. Cameron drank all that was in the metal cup. "There you go. The problem is nothing." The priest arched his brows.

"Nothing," said Cameron. "Then I guess we're done here."

The priest chuckled. "That's very good. Let me elaborate. The problem is what your new friends preach. That nothing matters. No church, no wealth, no property, all you need to do is be a good person and then," the priest raised his hands above his head, "you accept Him as your savior and all is OK."

"Doesn't sound too bad to me."

"No not too bad at all, for you, but what about civilization? What about the economies? The idea of being one with his Holy apart from all else," the priest wagged his finger, "it's very dangerous. Who would work? Who would farm?"

"You mean who would serve."

"Now, that's not nice." The priest nodded again to Peter. A swift slap came across Cameron's face. The priest kept speaking regardless of Cameron being struck. "If the truth of the pure ones got out, if the masses knew that truth, where would order be? Tell me."

Cameron spit blood to his side, "I don't need to tell you anything."

"Hmm," the priest nodded again and another blow landed to the side of Cameron's head. "You do need to tell me." The priest was no longer conversational. "You need to tell me where she is."

"I guess we're going to be here a long time," said Cameron.

Another blow. Cameron spit more blood.

CHAPTER 42
QUEBEC

Cameron heard two quick clicks behind him followed by two clinks of metal on the stone floor. Cameron did not need to see behind him to know from where those subtle sounds came. Pepe's handgun was a SIG Mosquito, based on the design of Cameron's P226. The Mosquito was ten percent smaller, the beauty of which was that with the silencer on, the only sound that could be heard when taking a shot was of the empty shell cartridges expelling.

Next to him, Cameron saw Peter for the first time, laid out on the floor chest down with two tight red holes through his head. Peter dropped so quickly that his blood had not had a chance to exit. The blood now pulsed out of him from a heart that was too late to catch up with the death of the brain.

"I wouldn't use that," said Pepe. Cameron could still not see his friend standing a few steps behind.

The priest said nothing and to Cameron's other side another man stepped backward into view. The big man was pointing the .357 he took off Cameron, not at Pepe, but at Cameron's head. The big man was without emotion and Cameron could tell that though man's eyes were fixed on

Pepe, the trigger of the gun was ready to be squeezed without hesitation.

"We'll do this the easy way," Cameron heard Pepe say. "You don't have to put down the gun."

"You're damn right I don't," said the big man. "You get any closer and your friend is done."

"I believe you," said Pepe. "I also believe you don't care if I leave with my friend or not. What you need to believe is that if I don't leave with my friend, no one will be leaving."

The big man slightly lowered the .357.

"It's OK, one thing at a time. Slowly put your thumb between the hammer," said Pepe.

The man slipped his thumb into the hammer of the .357 as Pepe requested.

"Now set it down," said Pepe.

The man set the .357 on the floor.

"Good. Now the coat."

The big man began to swiftly slip off his jacket.

"Slowly," said Pepe. The big man slowed, removed his jacket, and then let the coat drop to the floor.

Pepe stepped forward holding the mosquito to the man's stomach, his SIG 552 commando rifle hung clipped to his waist. With his free hand, Pepe frisked the big man to ensure he was clean.

"Nice, now untie my friend."

The man passed Pepe and went back out of Cameron's view. Pepe's mosquito followed the big man as Pepe turned toward Cameron and the priest. Cameron felt the big man tug at his bindings, tightening them at first, and then finally loosening them away from Cameron's wrists.

Cameron brought his wrists forward and began to rub them. He heard another clink on the stone floor and the thud of the big man collapsing behind him. The priest's eyes widened.

"Don't worry," said Pepe. "You're going to escort us out of here."

The priest nodded compliantly. Cameron stood and turned toward the door. He had not been sitting in the furnace room. The heat behind him came from a portable gas grill, flames licking through the grate, with at least a dozen more skewers of varying widths glowing red. Cameron looked back at the priest. The priest smiled and shrugged.

"Are you OK?" asked Pepe.

"A little sore, but I've been worse," said Cameron. He reached behind his back and pulled out his P226.

"All right, Monseigneur, get up from the stool. It's time to go," said Pepe.

The priest started to speak, "I am actually not a Monseigneur —" Pepe kicked the stool from under the priest and then said, "I don't really care if you are an altar boy. Now move it."

The priest had caught himself from falling onto the floor, stood up, and then smoothed out his black jacket.

The three walked out of the room into an arched hallway. Outside the door, two men were crumpled on the floor in pools of blood. Pepe gestured to the right, "What's down that way?"

"More crypts, a chapel, some storage," said the priest.

"Is there another way up to the cathedral? I don't want to go back the way I came," said Pepe.

"What is the way you came?" asked the priest.

"Through the back panel of the confessional booth like my friend."

Cameron now understood how he was taken below the church — a secret door in the confessional booth.

"Ah," said the priest, "that way you will find a stairwell that leads to a door near the dais and then continues up to the balcony."

Pepe kicked the shoulder of one of the dead men on the floor. The body shifted and then returned to its original position. "Will any of your friends be waiting for us?"

"I don't know what you mean," said the priest.

"Uh huh. Cameron, take the Monseigneur back to the confessional booth. Then wait for my signal."

Pepe slipped the mosquito into his waist, lifted the 552 rifle and left Cameron and the priest where they stood.

"You lead the way," said Cameron. He waved the end of the P226 from the priest toward the length of the hall and then to the priest again. The priest smiled and began to walk down the hall, leading Cameron to a bookcase. The priest lifted his arms to the side of the case. "Hold it," said Cameron. "What are you doing?"

The priest stopped reaching for the bookcase and left his arms suspended. "The passage is behind here."

"All right then, slowly." The priest rested his hands against the end of the bookcase and easily slid the case past an arched door. A light flickered on, revealing a set of stairs beginning at the archway. Cameron waved the priest up the stairs with his P226. "You fellas are unbelievable," said Cameron. Though Cameron had traveled this way shortly before, this was the first time he had actually had seen the hidden passage.

At the top of the steps was a series of wooden panels, the backs of the confessional booths. Cameron was sure that exiting from the wrong booth would be bad news for him. When Cameron scanned the room earlier he had thought the room looked clear. Pepe had obviously picked up on something since then.

The priest reached to open a panel.

"Just hold on for a moment," said Cameron.

"You know," said the priest, "it's not too late to work something out."

"It's not, hey?"

"Not at all. We have access to quite substantial resources. The million you requested for example."

"Yeah, I wanted to ask you, what denomination would that million be in?"

The priest grinned and then said, "Any denomination you like. Do you have a particular favorite?"

"I'd have to say that I am tossed between dollars and euros. Not long ago I would have said pounds, but the economy. It's a tricky thing."

The priest smirked. He knew that Cameron was playing with him. "You are making a big mistake, Mr. Kincaid."

"And that's another thing, you keep calling me Mr. Kincaid, not Cameron but Mr. Kincaid. How do you even know who I am?"

"We were at your restaurant. Sadly, we underestimated you. We were familiar with your celebrity on the Food Network—"

"You watch that?" asked Cameron.

"Doesn't everybody. We thought you were, well, not a problem. We did not anticipate this." The priest flashed a glance to the P226.

"Yeah, well, you think you know a guy."

Cameron's earpiece engaged. "I'm in position," said Pepe. The priest was obviously still unaware of the earpiece, as Pepe had taken him by surprise.

"OK, let's go," said Cameron.

The priest placed his hand on the panel and lightly pressed. Cameron heard a bolt slip and the panel swung open.

CHAPTER 43
QUEBEC

"You first," said Cameron.

The priest stepped into the booth and Cameron followed. As the priest opened the outer door he said, "You and your friend should really reconsider."

"Should we, now. C'mon, let's go."

"You are signing your own death warrant."

The priest stepped out of the confessional booth into the majesty of the cathedral. Cameron followed him.

"Keep walking," said Cameron. He pushed the barrel of the P226 into the small of the priest's back and then brought the butt back close to his own waist, shielding the gun under his jacket. The cathedral looked no different in appearance than the first time Cameron had walked through. People peppered the pews here and there, sunlight came in through the porticos, and that incense smell, almost nauseating, hung heavy. Pepe was nowhere to be seen, nor was anyone else that looked odd or suspicious. The priest led Cameron down the length of the pew and into the center aisle.

"Almost there. Let's mosey right out of here," said Cameron.

The priest began to lead Cameron down the aisle toward the entranceway of the cathedral. Cameron noticed the priest looking up to the balcony, looking for something or someone.

"Keep it moving," said Cameron.

The priest suddenly stopped, turned around to face Cameron, and then took a step backward. "This is your final chance. There will be no place to hide. I want her."

From the balcony over Cameron's shoulder came a low groan, and then a sniper rifle fell to the floor followed by a newly dead man.

"I don't think you will find her," said Cameron.

The priest looked up to the balcony to see Pepe.

Pepe held up an open palm to the priest and bent his fingers in a wave, his thumb holding a bloody Opinel penknife.

People began to stand and leave the pews, some whispering to each other, some distressed. Most just left silently.

The priest's face contorted and he let out a growl. "Kill them!" The priest quickly slipped his hand into his black jacket to grab a gun, only to be out-drawn by Cameron. However, as fast as the priest had thought and moved, Cameron did not have the burden of thinking to slow him down. Cameron acted on pure instinct. Cameron dove across the aisle to get cover behind a pew, firing his P226 at the priest while in motion. Before the priest had even pulled his gun from the holster beneath his jacket, Cameron's P226 had placed a bullet between the priest's awestruck eyes.

Cameron was not quick enough for another sniper who cracked off a shot at him during his dive for cover. A shot that was lucky for Cameron, unlucky for the sniper. The sniper missed his target, giving away his own position to Pepe. Pepe identified, targeted, and killed the sniper before he could get off a second shot.

At the door, an older man with baggy shorts and an

open guidebook froze as people exited around him. The man focused in the direction of Cameron, emotionless behind sunglasses. Baggy shorts saw Cameron lift his head from behind the pew, dropped the guidebook, and pulled a Ruger from under his shirt. Baggy fired two quick rounds toward Cameron. Cameron took a breath and then threw himself down to the floor of the aisle, twisting as he did so that when he hit the floor he was able to roll back on his shoulder, putting his gun in the general direction on the baggy shorts man. Cameron fired three rapid shots. The top of baggy short's skull separated from his head above his sunglasses. Baggy shorts dropped to his knees and then fell forward dead.

Cameron sat up and got to his knees. P226 still in hand, he twisted left and right, sweeping the room. "Clear," said Cameron. In his earpiece Pepe replied, "Clear."

"Than that's that. Let's move out."

Cameron spun around to the body of the dark priest behind him. The priest lay dead on his stomach. Cameron rolled the body over and pulled open the priest's jacket to check his inside pockets. Nothing. He grabbed the lapel and rolled the body back with a jerk. The priest's head thumped with a thud against the back of a pew. Cameron flipped the back of the jacket up and found what he was looking for sheathed in the priest's waistline, a Rex Mundi dagger. He transferred the dagger to his own waist.

"You're building up a collection, eh?" asked Pepe, already by Cameron's side. "I have two souvenirs myself," Pepe added, holding up two daggers. In Pepe's other hand, he held an open backpack. He dropped the daggers into the pack and then swept the room one more time before unclipping the 552 from the harness and adding the gun to the pack as well.

"Nice, let's go," said Cameron, his P226 still in hand.

At the end of the aisle, they stopped near the body of baggy shorts. The body was stretched out, face down, in a pool of blood and brains.

"Would you like this one?" asked Cameron. Pepe scowled and tilted his head curiously at the carnage and then shrugged, "You can have it. You made the mess after all."

Cameron stepped to the side of the torso. He could see that nothing was tucked into the back of the dead man, so he pushed the body over with his shoe. When the body rolled, lumps of brain oozed out of the gaping wound.

"Ew," said Pepe.

"It's nothing you haven't seen before," said Cameron.

"True."

"You remember that guard in Ghana? That was a mess." Cameron used his foot to slide the dead man's shirt up. In the waistband of the corpse's pants was the sheathed dagger Cameron was looking for.

"That was different, his head was sliced in half. This one, with the sunglasses still on, is very creepy to me."

Cameron took a moment to look at the ghastly face blindly staring back at the two of them. He tucked his P226 behind his back and said, "Yeah, he is creepy." Then in one motion, Cameron reached down with a swing of his arm, snatched the dagger, and took a step toward the door.

The people outside had already fled or were consoling each other in confusion beyond the promenade. None took notice of Cameron or Pepe as they made their way out of the church, down the steps, and into the small park across Rue Sainte-Felixine.

CHAPTER 44
QUEBEC

Cameron and Pepe approached the bench where Nicole sat with her legs crossed, her face basking in the sun. Her eyes were closed and they thought she had not heard them as they stepped in front of her.

With her eyes still closed, Nicole spoke, "You have only helped the operatives to their next lives."

"I feel better anyway," said Pepe.

"I have to agree," said Cameron. "Much better."

"There is no stopping Rex Mundi, for this is his world," Nicole brought her head down from basking in the sun and then slowly opened her eyes, "and his operatives are everywhere."

Nicole's eyes were vacant and had she not spoken, Cameron and Pepe would have thought her in a trance. Her gaze looked passed them. They turned toward each other and then out into the park where Nicole had fixed her stare.

At a hot dog cart directly across the clearing, a provincial police officer laughed at his partner for spilling sauce on his white uniform. The vendor, speaking quickly and waving a fistful of napkins and a bottle of water, was not getting either of the police officers' attention. Next to the hot dog stand, in front of the park fountain, a thin white-faced mime pushed his hands against the walls of an invisible box, the top and sides closing in on him, while two young couples watched his performance. Off to the side of the clearing, a group of college students were gathered on three blankets spread across the lawn for a picnic.

"You are saying all of these people are operatives?" asked Pepe.

"No," answered Cameron, "she is saying he is."

Behind the fountain, in a tweed cap, sunglasses, and T-shirt, stood a thin man looking back in their direction, his open smile gaping and familiar.

"You know that man?" asked Pepe, "Because he certainly seems to know you."

"His name is Christophe," said Cameron. He smiled back at Christophe, bowed his head, and then asked Nicole, "How long has he been watching you?"

"Not long after you left. I pretended I did not know he was there," said Nicole.

"Good girl. Well, he knows we know now," said Cameron.

"Uh," said Pepe, "so what are we to do?" He too smiled in Christophe's direction.

"Well it's his dumb luck those two policemen are standing so close," said Cameron.

"Or his misfortune," said Pepe.

"His misfortune?" asked Nicole.

"Pepe's right," Cameron said. "Christophe cannot take action anymore than we can."

Pepe spoke in a low voice, eyes still focused on Christophe. "Nicole, dear, gather your things. We need to move quickly."

Cameron added, "I don't think he has anyone left to call."

"I don't want to find out." Pepe looked down at Nicole, "Now, my dear, let's go."

Magazines were stacked beside Nicole and a sketchpad was on her lap. She had brought the magazines at Cameron's behest so that she could blend more easily in the park. The sketchpad was added after Nicole had continually insisted that she needed her mind to stay pure. Now Nicole stood, leaving everything except her bag on the bench.

CHAPTER 45
QUEBEC

"OK, this way," said Cameron as he waved goodbye to Christophe, "as we discussed." Cameron led the others down the sidewalk. They had discussed an escape route on the slim chance they would be pursued by the Rex Mundi or the police. Though neither of those things had happened, this third scenario was applicable as a reason to initiate the plan.

The three walked briskly through the park without turning around to look back.

"Is he still following?" asked Nicole as they neared the street.

"I'm sure of it," said Cameron. "He would not be allowed to let you slip out of his hands a second time."

"I guess you are right," said Nicole.

"Stay between Pepe and myself, it will be over soon."

"Is there another way? You know I detest violence."

Pepe answered for Cameron, "There is no other way. *Ce qui sera, sera.*"

The three waited on the curb for the light to change and then crossed the street. Cameron led them down the sidewalk to the corner where they turned, and then up the street passed a jeweler and a café. Between the café and the next building was a small alley, only wide enough for two. The alley led to a parking lot behind the street side shops.

Cameron stopped them in front of the café.

"Wait for it, wait for it," said Cameron.

"Wait for what?" asked Nicole.

Pepe replied, "You will see. Our friend Christophe needs to take the bait."

"Wait for it," said Cameron a third time. Nicole realized now that Cameron was looking at the metal napkin dispenser to see the reflection of the corner behind them.

Christophe was not far behind and would soon be making the corner.

In a softer tone Cameron said, "OK, now." He quickly led Pepe and Nicole into the alley.

Christophe saw them dart into the café-side alley and followed them. When he reached the back of the building, he found the large parking area. Christophe stayed inside the mouth of the alley. He peeked out into the parking area and was unable to see Nicole and the men right away. A large planter at the mouth of the opening blocked his view. He stuck his head out farther to get a better look. Still unable to find where they had gone, Christophe took a few steps out into the open. Up to the right, he finally saw Cameron and Nicole. Christophe reached into his waist and pulled out a large black .44 magnum. In the secluded parking lot away from the park, he was confident he could use the heavy weapon the other operatives had given him.

Christophe tried to pull back the slide as he had been shown. Because he was nervous, he could not remember exactly what to squeeze.

In Christophe's ear came a voice. "Let me help you with that." He felt a sharp pressure on his throat and let his hand go limp as Pepe gently removed the useless metal from his grip.

In Christophe's excitement, he did not notice that the

dark-haired man had split off from the other two. The large planter with the huge bush at the mouth of the alley that had hid Christophe from the parking area also shielded Pepe from his view. When Christophe had stepped out into the lot he had walked right past Pepe.

"Let me go, please. Please. I will disappear. You will not see me again," said Christophe.

"If I let you go, you will leave and not return to your friends?" asked Pepe.

Christophe's gaping open smile returned to his face, "*Oui,* yes, yes."

"I'm sorry," said Pepe, "I do not believe you." With a sudden thrust, Pepe pushed the tip of his Opinel into Christophe's throat, at once severing his jugular and puncturing his larynx.

Christophe's knees went weak and his hands wrapped his throat to block the sputtering blood. Pepe squeezed his shoulders to support him and gently backed him up to the building. Pepe slowly stepped backwards while his eyes scanned the parking lot for witnesses. There were none. When Pepe felt the wall on their backs, he gently eased Christophe down to a sitting position then kneeled in front of him.

Blood already soaked Christophe's T-shirt and he gasped for breath. His sunglasses had fallen off when Pepe had set him down and now his eyes stared wide at Pepe, still pleading. Christophe tried to speak, releasing only scarlet bubbles and short, high-pitched wheezes.

Pepe said in a soft voice, "Do not try to speak. I would make it short for you, and I am sure you would like me to. I cannot." Christophe held one hand away from his throat, impotently grasping at Pepe. Pepe did not flinch, safely out of Christophe's reach.

"Now, now," said Pepe. "You know why I cannot. Cameron told me you were a traitor. That because of you many people died."

Christophe rested the arm that he had taken such effort

to claw toward Pepe. His eyes also rested, no longer wide.

"You will go fast enough," said Pepe. "Use this time to think about your mistakes. It builds character." Pepe patted Christophe atop his tweed cap, stood, and then walked away.

CHAPTER 46
QUEBEC

Pepe slid into the backseat, "So."

"I promised Marie that I would take Nicole to Nova Scotia," said Cameron. "I think that will finally be the last stop."

"I will go with you," said Pepe.

"I would like that."

Nicole turned toward the backseat. In her hands, she held up a Canadian highway atlas. "I know the way to the retreat in Nova Scotia."

"I am sure you do, *demoiselle,*" said Pepe.

"I am glad somebody does," said Cameron.

Nicole ran her finger down the indexed list of provinces. When she found the page she was looking for, she opened the atlas to the provincial map of Nova Scotia. "We need to get here," said Nicole. She lifted the book for both men to see and pointed to a field of white in southern Nova Scotia, not far from the ocean. "Once we are here, I know I can get us the rest of the way."

Cameron did not challenge her or care to. He knew that she was incapable of lying, and whether or not Nicole really could get them there, she believed she could.

CHAPTER 47
THE CATHARI TREASURE

"Then it is true. *Je le savais,*" said Pepe.

"What is?" asked Cameron. They were a few hours out of Quebec driving into the indigo dusk.

"*Les Chevaliers du Christ,* they really exist."

"Chevaliers, Knights, The Knights of Christ. Lady Mani, the old woman back in Toronto, she called me a *chevalier.*" Cameron rattled his fingertips off into a series of taps against the steering wheel, "So did Marie."

"*Les Chevaliers du Christ,* you know, that is another name for *Les Templiers.* You said Marie told you that brotherhood we are going to meet are Knights whose order have been caretakers of the treasure in times of strife for 800 years," said Pepe.

"That's what she told me."

"My *grand-mère* told me that many of the people of Acadia were descended from *Les Templiers,* the Knights of Christ."

"What are you talking about?" asked Cameron.

"Have you been living under a rock? Everyone knows of *Les Templiers,* the Knights Templar. The books, the movies.... Really, Cameron, you should get out of the restaurant more often."

"You got me there," said Cameron.

"*Grand-mère* told me that the Knights of Christ were fathers of Acadia, the part that is now Nova Scotia, long before the area was settled by other French or the British. She said the British forced everyone to take an oath of allegiance and those that did not fled to other parts of Canada, some to Louisiana, all descended from the Knights of Christ."

"Yeah, well. After the last few days I am not the least bit surprised," said Cameron.

"Fascinating," said Pepe, his voice becoming distant.

"Sure," said Cameron, unimpressed.

"Ah, but you see," Pepe lifted his hands above his head and then dropped them on his lap, "of course you don't see."

Cameron adjusted the rearview to look Pepe in the eyes, "See what."

"If that part is true, then the other part my *grand-mère* told me may also be true."

"And that is?" asked Cameron.

"The Knights fled from Europe when they were being persecuted," Pepe paused for a second and then locked eyes with Cameron, "and with them they brought a treasure."

Cameron cocked his brow, looked at the road, and then back to Pepe. "Are you saying what I think you're saying?"

"Am I saying what you think I am saying? *Tu êtes ridicule.* You know that is what I am saying. For centuries people have been guessing what the treasure was and where they hid it." Pepe gestured to the young woman sitting in front of him, "I am saying that people have been guessing wrong. The treasure is not an it, the treasure is a she."

"That's ridiculous," Cameron shook his head, "you read too many conspiracy books."

"No, no, I believe this could be true. You said so

yourself. Marie told you that Nicole is the treasure that can change the world."

"I don't know," said Cameron.

"It is as Mr. Pepe says," said Nicole. They had thought she had dozed off as she had been facing the window quietly since they left Quebec.

"It is?" asked Cameron.

"Yes. Long ago, in the old country, *Les Templiers* and *les bonnes gens,* the Cathar, lived together and supported each other. The Languedoc was advanced in thought and education. The Catholic Church, however, after years of corruption, became a puppet of Rex Mundi. They thought the Cathar threatened their church. They believed that if they did not control the knowledge of faith that their church would suffer. The nobles of the north also were prey to Rex Mundi. They saw the wealth of the region, the wealth of *Les Templiers* and wanted it for their own. In the year 1209, the nobles of the north and the Catholics joined forces to rid themselves of the Cathar, to take what was the Cathar's, and to keep people from learning the true way to purity. Over the course of twenty years, a great crusade swept through the Occitan, followed by twenty years of the Inquisition. You have heard of this?" Nicole turned her head from the window to Cameron and Pepe, both fixated on her story.

"Yes," said Pepe, "I know of the Inquisition."

"Yes, of course," said Cameron, his thigh still sore from the skewers, "go on."

Nicole continued, "By that time, except for very few strongholds, all of the towns and forts supporting the Cathar had fallen. The greatest of these was the fort at Montségur, atop the mountain, high above the valleys. Ten thousand crusaders held siege on the fortress for almost a year. The attackers persisted because they believed that those who held Montségur held with them the legendary Treasure of the Cathar. Down to less than 400 defenders, the Cathar at Montségur finally agreed to surrender. A two-week truce stopped all fighting and it looked like there would be a peaceful outcome. However, when the two weeks passed more than 200 Cathar, Parfait and Credentes, were brutally forced down the mountain and burned alive."

"200 people?" asked Cameron.

"Yes, they were put into a wooden, I don't know the word, palissade maybe," Nicole looked at Pepe.

"Prison, they put them into a wooden prison. A stockade," said Pepe.

"*Oui,* a stockade. They force all 200 people into the stockade to burn to death."

Cameron anxiously asked Nicole, "And what about the other 200? You said there were 400 Cathar in the fort."

"Those left in the fort watched this burning. They were the supporters of the Cathar. The attackers believed they had taken all of the Cathar and destroyed them. Four Parfaits stayed hidden in the fort at this time. Then the next night, with the help of those left in the fort, these Parfaits secretly escaped by climbing ropes down the flat mountainside. The foolish operatives of Rex Mundi believed that the wealth of the Cathar and Templars had been secretly coming out of the fort over the time of the siege. When they learned of the great escape they decided that the greatest treasure had gone with them down those ropes in the dark."

"And it did," said Pepe, "not gold or worthless relics. It was the Parfaits themselves that were the treasure."

"That is correct," said Nicole. "Those that held the fort said that the Cathar and Templar took with them their ark of the covenant, or the Holy Grail, things that mean nothing to the Cathar. What escaped that night was the direct line to Christ and the Holy Spirit. The true treasure is purity and salvation."

"And of the knights?" asked Pepe. "How did they get here?"

"The Cathar were hid among Les Templiers for the next fifty years. The nobles and the church became further possessed by the greed of Rex Mundi. They no longer needed the Chevaliers du Christ. The nobles wanted the lands and wealth of Les Templiers. The king wanted the great treasure most of all. The French king and nobles killed two popes to get an operative of Rex Mundi in power. Then, to put their evil plan in action, they set a trap for Les Templiers. All over France secret sealed orders were given to the king's men. When the time came, the orders were unsealed and the trap was sprung. Everywhere Les Templiers were arrested and all of their property taken in the name of the king. The king was disappointed, though. Even in his surprise attack, the great treasure of Les Templiers, the treasure of the Cathar, eluded his grasp."

"To the world the story ends there," said Pepe. "What happened to the treasure of the Templars remains a mystery."

"Not to the Rex Mundi. They fuel the world with disinformation to help them in their conquest," said Nicole.

"Hmm." Pepe pressed his lips together and peered out into the darkness that now blanketed the outside of the car.

"The attack was not totally unexpected. Some Chevaliers knew the betrayal was to come. It was inevitable that the operatives of Rex Mundi would strike, as that is the way of Rex Mundi. Measures had already begun to secure the order and the treasure. From across France, wagons brought Les Templiers and their papers to their ships in La Rochelle. Not all of the Chevaliers made it out so when word came of the others' arrest, those gathered with the Cathar in La Rochelle fled France, eventually settling in what is now called Nova Scotia. That was seven centuries ago."

"La Rochelle?" asked Pepe.

"*Oui,* Monsieur Laroque," said Nicole.

Pepe lightly sighed and raised his brows.

Nicole had finished her story as quickly as she had started. She turned her head back out the window. The Chevy was now going south down the border of Maine and she could see a peach ribbon in the distant west where the night had not yet stolen the sky.

"So it is true, then," said Pepe, looking west as well.

"So it is," said Cameron.

CHAPTER 48
NOVA SCOTIA

After riding in the Chevy for nine hours, Cameron looked forward to the six-hour sleep ahead of him. The ferry would not be crossing from Saint John to Digby until morning. Now the ferry terminal, and most everything else in Saint John, was dark. Nicole and Pepe had been sleeping since Pepe's turn to drive three or four hours ago, though Pepe would grunt on occasion to let Cameron know he was alert enough if needed.

Cameron parked the Chevy near the ferry dock. He rubbed his eyes and then opened the door to get some fresh air. The smell of the Bay of Fundy was thick as the mist floated inland from the shore. If there were stars or a moon in the sky, it was a mystery to Cameron. The only light he could see was the misted glow of a white halogen on the eave of the terminal and in the rearview mirror, the brighter, more defined lights of the gas station.

Cameron thought about walking the block to the gas station to see if there was anything to eat or drink. His coffee-laden gut dissuaded him from getting out of the car. The decision to buy the black, tarry elixir at their last stop had come out of desperation and had begun to haunt him soon afterward.

If he closed his eyes and breathed in deeply, the moisture in the mist alone would be enough to sedate him. Still, something about being near the ocean exhilarated him, even as tired as he was.

* * * * *

A marker for Kejimkujic National Park broke the tree line. The sign was the first road marker other than the Route 8 signs that had intermittently popped up since turning off 101 in Clementine.

The ferry had landed in Digby an hour ago and they were already in the heart of Nova Scotia.

"We are close," said Nicole. She unclasped the necklace and removed the pendant from around her neck. The pendant's dark emerald swallowed all of the light that hit the gem's dull surface, encapsulating in the emerald's center as a muted green fire. Cameron watched as Nicole used her fingernails to pick at the seam where the green gem joined the metal setting.

"I wanted to ask you about that," said Cameron.

"What did you want to ask?" replied Nicole, as she spun the setting, trying to pry the metal scrolling at the emerald's edge from different angles.

"I was surprised that the necklace was so significant to Marie. I mean, given that it is a physical object and all."

"This pendant is special because…" with a snap Nicole twisted the large gem away from the antique backing and held the now bare metal up to Cameron to show him what lay behind the stone, "it is a key."

Across Nicole's palm, the pendant was splayed open. The emerald was still connected to the setting by a hinge and on the back of the gem and the face of the ancient setting was an image. Engraved clearly and lightly in the metal of the setting's face was a diamond-shaped diagram. Above the diamond to the side was set a tiny emerald chip.

A thin line ran from the center of the diamond to the chip. Another engraved line led out of the center of the diamond diagram toward the large emerald, a deeper thicker line.

The Canadian highway atlas was on the seat between Cameron and Nicole, still opened to the provincial map of southern Nova Scotia. She placed the pendant on the map and centered the emerald on an island in the Medway River. Nicole spun the setting to the left until the line between the diamond and emerald chip were pointing at Bangs Falls to the northwest. Cameron could see that the second line, the deeper thicker line, pointed toward the north side of Kejimkujic National Park, right about what Cameron judged to be their current location. Nicole traced the lighter line from the center of the diamond toward the little emerald chip at the edge and continued past the pendant by making an invisible line to a place on the map that satisfied her.

"It's very close," said Nicole, "you will want to slow down."

"You're telling me that pendant corresponds to our map?" asked Pepe. He had watched Nicole place the pendant on the map and use the makeshift device the same way Cameron and he were trained to use lensatic compasses in the Legion. The difference was that their military field compasses had magnetized needles. Nicole's decoder did not have a way of telling true north that Pepe could see, and he did not see how she knew her bearings without a magnetized needle.

"It only needs to give me the general direction. I will know what it is I am looking for when I see it," said Nicole.

The corners of Pepe's mouth dropped to form an upside-down smile. Pepe realized that the scale of the map, large or small, did not matter if whoever was decoding with the key knew what they were looking for. The pendant truly was a key, and a good one, that could be used with any map that had the correct landmarks.

"There," said Nicole. She pointed at a line on the map designating a two-track utility road. "That is where we need to turn."

The road came up quickly, as Nicole predicted. Though Cameron had been driving slowly, he did not see the two-track until the Chevy was upon the road. There were no signs and they drove past before braking. The mouth to the two-track was overgrown and could easily have been mistaken for an old logging trail.

Cameron stopped the Chevy, backed up to the mouth of the two-track, and then turned off Route 8 onto the overgrown utility road.

The Chevy plodded over the old road for some time. Regardless of how gently Cameron tried to maneuver, the deep weatherworn dips rolled their stomachs. Sections of the two-track were so crowded by brush and fallen branches that Cameron had to stop several times so that he and Pepe could clear the path. They continued at a slow pace until, a far distance from the main road, the evergreens turned to hardwoods, and the two-track became a groomed dirt road.

Cameron looked into the rearview at Pepe. Pepe shrugged in response.

They had driven for another fifteen minutes when Pepe leaned forward between Nicole and Cameron. "In the trees," said Pepe. He pointed to the tree line to the left of the Chevy. Cameron slowed to a crawl so that he could peer into the woods. Behind the tree line, visible in some places, hidden in others, a wooden split-rail fence ran parallel with the road. From what they could see, the fence was an amalgam of new and aged rails ranging from barn-wood black and grey to fresh-cut blonde. Many of the posts had fresh dirt mounds near their base no more than a few winters old. For being in the middle of the forest, the fence was very well maintained.

Not much farther past where Pepe first saw glimpses of the split-rail fence, the Chevy came to a lane that veered up a slight grade toward an opening in the trees. At the top of the grade stood a tall wrought-iron gate, blocking the entrance to a clearing behind. The gate and its two tall supporting stone pillars seemed out of place between the split-rail fences that squeezed the portal on either side.

"Something's back here," said Cameron.

CHAPTER 49
NOVA SCOTIA

"We are here," said Nicole. "Please stop the car."

Cameron did as Nicole requested and stopped the Chevy in the middle of the road. Nicole stepped out of the Chevy before Cameron had even switched off the ignition. She walked around the front of the Chevy toward the gate. Cameron got out and joined Nicole. The two stood silently between the Chevy and the gate.

Pepe shifted across the backseat toward his door. He wanted to join Cameron and Nicole outside of the Chevy. He stopped when he saw a young man in a canvas jacket come out of the trees, rifle tucked under his arm, steps ahead of where the Chevy had stopped. The man was dressed like a hunter. Pepe thought there was something odd about the man and decided to stay where he was. As the hunter stepped onto the road, another young man wearing the same type of canvas jacket came out from the trees across the road from the first. The second man had a rifle tucked under his arm as well. The two hunters paired up in front of the Chevy and then wordlessly approached Cameron and Nicole.

Without moving his upper body, Pepe pulled the

mosquito from under his shirt.

Nicole turned to the men as they closed in and lightly bowed her head, the hunters responded in kind. Nicole said to Cameron, "These men are my friends. They will watch over me."

"Hello," said Cameron. He tapped his pant leg with the tips of his fingers. Pepe recognized the subtle gesture. The finger tap was a signal to lower the mosquito that Cameron knew was just out of sight. The two hunters did not verbally respond to Cameron, choosing to offer the same slight bow they had exchanged with Nicole, instead. Cameron nodded back. When Cameron's head was bowed he noticed that the hunters were each wearing an emerald ring in the same style as Nicole's pendant, except their rings also had a symbol on them that Cameron recognized. Cameron had seen the familiar symbol for the first time only a few days before and now understood the significance. The emerald green tiepins worn by the bodyguards in the library of Le Dragon Vert had been embossed with the same small design.

The young hunters turned toward the gate in unison, walked over, and then stopped to wait for Nicole.

Nicole faced Cameron, "I cannot thank you enough, Mr. Kincaid. You are *un bon homme,* a good man," Nicole glanced at Pepe sitting in the back seat, "so is Mr. Pepe." Nicole smiled at Pepe and he responded with a quick wink and a nod. She turned back to Cameron, "You should live your life more purely, but do not worry too much if you cannot. You will have a better chance in your next life, without the hardships that you have had to endure in this one."

"I will do my best," said Cameron. He wondered if Nicole somehow knew something about his past and then let the thought pass. "You try to stay out of trouble yourself."

"*Au revoir,* Mr. Kincaid," said Nicole. She walked toward the gate to join the two young men. As she approached the hunters, one of them opened a small panel on the stone pillar revealing a numeric keypad. The hunter tapped in a code and a buzz came from the panel followed by metallic thud inside the gate. The other hunter pushed the heavy wrought-iron door open.

Nicole stepped behind the gate and then turned back toward Cameron and Pepe and gave a gentle wave. She waited there and watched the two men return to the Chevy, turn the car around, and start back toward Route 8.

Cameron did not look into the rearview mirror as he drove back down the dirt road. There was no real reason to look back. Cameron knew that the gate would disappear from view as quickly as they had found the mysterious portal. Whatever was hidden behind those iron doors was hidden well. Cameron had promised that he would get Nicole to safety and he was satisfied that she would be safe with this order of men living out in the woods. Nicole was a treasure after all.

CHAPTER 50
NOVA SCOTIA, TUESDAY, 1330 HOURS

Cameron and Pepe stopped to fuel up in Clementine before turning onto 101. Pepe stood at the old gas pump outside of Cameron's window watching the numbers roll by as he filled the Chevy with gas.

Cameron took his cell phone off the seat and tapped the power on. Nothing happened — he had nursed the cell phone battery as far as possible. Cameron rolled down the window and waved the cell phone in front of Pepe. "This thing is dead. Any juice left in yours?"

Pepe slipped his hand in his pocket and then took out his phone for Cameron.

"This thing is ancient," said Cameron. He turned the old clamshell phone as if he had not seen one in years. "Does it even work?"

"Ha, ha," said Pepe. "It works."

"This thing is an antique." Cameron flipped open the clamshell and the screen lit up. "No color? I don't believe it."

"Less features is longer battery," said Pepe, his brow stern. "Now do you want to use it?"

"Yeah, yeah, relax," said Cameron.

"Don't complain," said Pepe.

Cameron winked at Pepe and Pepe flashed a smile back. These men had been friends for so long they had become brothers.

Cameron rapidly dialed a number and waited for the other end to pick up.

"Hello," said a voice. The voice was Claude, another old friend and brother.

"Claude, hey there, it's Cameron."

"I have not heard from you. Are you OK?"

"Yeah, I'm fine. I'll be coming back right after I return Pepe to Montreal."

"Pepe is there with you?"

"Sure, he says hello." Cameron gave Pepe a knowing glance.

"*Bonjour, mon ami*," said Pepe. Cameron continued, "He says *bonjour*."

"I heard him," said Claude. "*Bonjour*."

Cameron looked up at Pepe again. "Claude says *bonjour*." Pepe gave a small wave to the phone accompanied with the same smile he had flashed at Cameron a moment before.

"So you will be back soon?"

"Yes, Claude, and thank you for covering. I'm sure a lot of people have been asking questions about the other night."

"Funny thing," said Claude, "no one is asking questions."

* * * * *

THE END

CAMERON KINCAID RETURNS IN *THE SOMALI DECEPTION*

ABOUT THE AUTHOR

Daniel Arthur Smith is the author of the international bestsellers ***THE CATHARI TREASURE, THE SOMALI DECEPTION***, and a few other novels and short stories.

He was raised in Michigan and graduated from Western Michigan University where he studied meta-physics, cognitive science, philosophy, and comparative religion. He began his career as a bartender, barista, poetry house proprietor, teacher and then became a technologist and futurist for the Fortune 100 across the Americas and Europe.

Daniel has traveled to over 300 cities in 22 countries, residing in Los Angeles, Kalamazoo, Prague, Crete, and now writes in Manhattan where he lives with his wife and young sons.

For more information, visit **danielarthursmith.com**

STAY IN THE LOOP

Following your favorite authors on Facebook, Twitter, or other social media has become a sketchy business. Facebook and other companies block authors from conversing regularly with readers unless they are willing to cough up BIG BUX to 'promote' every post. To make sure you are receiving the latest updates, freebies, and stories on everything in the Daniel Arthur Smith universe you have to join his email newsletter. As a subscriber, you'll receive early Advance Review Copies (ARCS) of all of Daniel's books and stories… for free! In addition to all of that, Daniel regularly gives away lots of other loot like signed books and posters, so make certain that you are subscribed.

Printed in Great Britain
by Amazon

32905757R00119